Sweet Summertime Wishes

A SMALL-TOWN SINGLE DAD ROMANCE

TIA MARLEE

A NOVEL CHOICE

A NOVEL CHOICE PRESS

Contents

To my loving family who have cheered me on every step of the way.

CHAPTER ONE

Daniel

I SMILE AND PAT Brant's shoulder as I take my place beside him as his best man. In just a few short months, he's gone from bachelor to family man. I'm happy for him. I am.

I think back to the day that Heather and I got married. It was a bigger affair than Brant and Morgan's back yard wedding, unfortunately. I wanted nothing more than to elope, but Heather's family wouldn't hear of it. Appearances and all that.

Instead of folding chairs, potted plants, and twinkling lights strung about the back yard, we were in a hall decorated with so much tulle it looked like the craft store had a clearance sale.

By the time that shindig was over, my feet ached, and I'd started to wonder if my life would always be dictated by grand expectations. Glancing over to the chairs lined up in front of me, I smile. My marriage wasn't all bad, though. Elli is the love of my life. That girl came into the world like a whirlwind, and has lived that way ever since.

I turn my attention back to the house in time to see Morgan step through the sliding glass door with Susan. Dressed in a beautiful white gown that fans out just around the bottom, she looks radiant. Just how a bride should look on her wedding day.

I take a peek at Brant and see him discreetly wiping tears from the corners of his eyes. Man, he's got it bad. Can't say I blame him. Morgan and her son Liam are amazing people, and Brant's been a happier man since she gave him a shot. All he's ever wanted is standing at the end of that aisle.

Elli's wiggling captures my attention. I send her a *be still* look, and she smiles sweetly. She has me wrapped around her little finger, and she knows it. She could get away with almost any-thing—almost. A beautiful redhead moves from the row behind, up to the open seat beside Elli and leans down to whisper into her ear.

Elli nods her head and turns to watch as Liam brings Morgan up the aisle. Following her gaze, I smile at the sight of six-year-old Liam walking slowly toward Brant. That kid never moves at a normal pace, which goes to show how serious he's taking his wedding duties.

My eyes are drawn back to the redhead who is craning her neck to see. A smile pulling at her plump red lips. Who is this woman and why have I never seen her before? She is all long legs and curves squeezed into a one piece pant suit, a deep green that seems to match her eyes. Her strappy little sandals show off toenails painted a rich red. She's gorgeous.

She looks like relationship material, and I do not do relation-ships. I've got no interest in getting my heart broken again. Mystery woman will have to remain just that. A mystery. I force myself to look away and pay attention to the ceremony taking place.

Brant and Morgan link hands, and the officiant begins speaking. My eyes keep darting back to where the redhead is now dabbing her eyes with a tissue. I've never understood how women get so emotional at someone else's wedding. I turn my attention back to the happy couple.

A few minutes later, vows are said, rings are exchanged, and the officiant pronounces Brant and Morgan husband and wife. Brant dips her and gives her a kiss that borders on inappropriate, causing their guests to break into laughter. Shaking my head at his antics, I just smile. Good for him.

The guests all file into the house, leaving the happy family, myself, and Susan to do the after-ceremony pictures. The photographer calls us over and takes a million shots with different poses before letting Susan and me go. She wants to take some of the new family. Memories.

"What a beautiful wedding." Susan sighs as we make our way back to the house for the mini reception. Her flowy, pale pink bridesmaids dress is a bit too long, causing her to walk slowly so as not to trip.

I hold out my arm in case she needs something to grip. "It was," I agree. I have no idea what else to say. Weddings are not really my deal. Especially after the fiasco that was my marriage and subsequent divorce. No thanks. I'd rather stay single.

Sam, Susan's husband, meets us as we approach the house. "Watch your step, dear," he says, taking Susan by the arm. I swear they are like an old married couple, but they can't be much older than me.

I pause to let them enter the house before I step inside to find Elli. I spot her across the open kitchen. She is animatedly talking about something, blocking whomever she's held captive with her storytelling, when rich laughter stops me dead in my tracks. The throaty sound sends sparks shooting across my whole body.

Moving further into the room, I see her. Head tipped back, laughter springing from those beautiful lips. A sudden urge to grab her and kiss her hits me. Before I know what I am doing, I find myself standing in front of her.

"Daddy," Elli says, turning toward me. "There you are!"

I turn my attention to my daughter and smile. Thank goodness she's here, or I'd have jumped right off the cliff into the deep end with one very tempting redhead with emerald green eyes.

"Hey, pumpkin, having a good time?" I chance another look at the pretty woman who's smiling from ear to ear.

"Elli is wonderful," she says. "She was telling me about the fishing trip the two of you went on last year. Did you really lose a fishing pole in the lake?" She laughs again softly.

"Oh," I say, blushing a bit. "Yeah, Elli here didn't want to bring the poor fish in, so she just let go." I chuckle. "I tried to go in after it, but the fish took off, dragging the pole behind."

Elli is laughing behind her hand now. "You were a big ole mess," she giggles.

"And whose fault was that, little missy?" I ask, tickling her.

"Yours!" she squeals. "If you didn't tell me we were going to eat him for dinner, I wouldn't have let go."

I stop tickling and stare at her. "What did you think we were fishing for?" I ask incredulously.

"Fun," she says simply as she shrugs her shoulders.

"Fun," I repeat, putting her back onto her feet. "Elli girl, you are something else."

"Tell you a secret," Red says, whispering loudly. "I don't particularly like eating the catch either." She glances around the room. "I'm going to go tell the newlyweds congratulations," she says, standing. "It was nice to meet you, Elli and . . ."

"Daniel," I say quickly, realizing I had never given her my name.

"Well, it was nice to meet you, Elli and Daniel. I'm sure I'll see you again." She stands and walks towards the kitchen where Morgan and Brant have just come in with Liam.

"Can I go play with Liam?" Elli asks, looking up at me with her big blue eyes the color of Texas Bluebonnets.

As if I could tell her no. "Sure." I'm glad Elli and Liam get along. Brant and Evan are about the only friends I have these days. Having Liam around gives Elli someone to play with when she's with me.

I watch as Elli beelines to Liam and grabs his hand. They head to the corner of the living room where Brant has set up a play area. Before long, the two are playing with the cars on the electric race track Liam got for Christmas.

Turning, I head into the kitchen to give the bride and groom my well wishes. There by the island stands Evan, talking to none other than my beautiful Red.

Wait. What? No, she isn't mine. I don't do relationships, and I'm definitely not into the redhead with the throaty laugh and curves in all the right places. Evan can have her. She's got to be closer to his age, anyway.

"Congratulations," I say, kissing Morgan on the hand before stepping back and clapping Brant on the back. "It was a beautiful wedding."

"Thanks!" Morgan looks at Brant with nothing but love in her eyes. "I can't believe you pulled all this off!" she says, laughing.

"Well, I had some help," Brant says sheepishly. "Our friends helped me organize everything so all you would have to do is get ready and say I do."

"He owes us all a cookout," I say, shooting Morgan a wink.

Brant clears his throat and rubs his hand along the back of his neck. "Let us get them moved in, and then I'll invite you over."

Morgan grins. "I love you," she whispers before going up on her toes to plant a kiss on his smiling face.

"I love you too," he says proudly.

The sound of laughter has me whipping my head around toward Evan and my Red.

I can't take my eyes off of her. Evan leans forward and puts his hand on her arm.

Nope.

Nope. Nope. Nope.

Not gonna happen.

I stalk over and tap him on the shoulder. "Evan, can I talk to you for a minute?" I interrupted them, but I don't care. Red looks amused, her eyebrow pulled up and a half smile on her lips.

"Uh, sure man, what's up?" he asks, his brows drawn in confusion.

"In the garage, please?" I ask, dragging him away from her.

"Excuse us." He mumbles something about being right back, but he won't be. Not if I can help it.

We step into the garage, and I turn and face him. "Whoa, D, what's got you all worked up man?" Evan stands with his hands up.

Rolling my shoulders I try to relax. "Sorry, Ev, I don't know what the heck came over me. I saw you talking to Red and snapped." Shame bites at me. What in the world just happened? Sinking onto the bench near the door, I put my head in my hands.

"Oh," Evan sighs, running his hand through his thick dark hair. "You *like* her." It's a statement, not a question.

"Nope," I say, shaking my head. "I don't do relationships, remember." If only I could get my hormones to agree with my head here.

"Cool," he says slowly. "So you're good if I ask her out?" I look up to see a huge grin plastered across his smug face.

"Do it, and I'll sink your keys in the lake," I mutter.

He laughs, grabbing his stomach. "Man, you are funny. No wonder you don't date—you'd lose your mind." Still laughing, he turns and grabs the doorknob. "If you like her, ask her out. What do you have to lose?"

He opens the door and steps back inside, leaving me to my traitorous thoughts.

He makes it sound simple. Like asking her out wouldn't violate my "no women except Elli" rule. I don't think I was in love with Heather anymore when we decided to divorce, but I know it hurt to lose that relationship. The family I worked so hard to build. I vowed never to get myself into that situation again. Hence, the "no relationships" rule.

Red's laughter floats through the door and into my heart. For the first time I question my self-imposed single life.

Stepping back into the kitchen, I take a deep breath and plaster a smile on my face. Evan has distanced himself from Red, but nods in my direction as if to encourage me to break my own rule.

Wiping my hands on my pants, I make my way back over to where Red is now talking with Susan and her husband, Sam. As I stand between Sam and Red, I try to focus on the conversation, but I can't help sneaking glances at Red.

"Wasn't it a beautiful wedding, Daniel?" Susan asks.

"I didn't get your name before," I blurt. I can feel heat travel to my cheeks. Susan laughs and Sam slides his hand through her arm and guides her away from us.

"Oh." Red giggles. "Reese," she says, reaching up and putting a stray strand of glorious silky hair behind her ear. "I'm Morgan's co-teacher. How do you know the couple?"

Reese. Unique. I like it. I realize she asked me a question and scramble to come up with the right answer. "Um, I'm friends with

Brant," I say in a rush. "Listen, Reese, I was wondering—" A strong hand lands on my shoulder.

"Daniel," Brant says. "I just want to thank you again for helping me make this happen. Couldn't have done it without you, man." Brant needed a kick in the pants to face his feelings for Morgan, and I was happy to give it.

"No problem, boss," I say, chuckling. "Maybe one day you can return the favor." I wink to let him know that I'm joking. He looks from me, to Reese, and back again before raising an eyebrow and smiling.

"Maybe so," he says, before clapping me on the shoulder and walking away again.

Susan and Sam have drifted over to where Elli and Liam are playing in the living room. The other guests, mostly teachers Morgan works with, mingle around the food that's been laid out on trays in some fancy design.

Brant's interruption is enough time to remind me, I don't date. Especially younger, beautiful women. I shake my head and squeeze the back of my neck. What was I thinking—of course I can't break my rule.

"You were saying?" Reese asks.

"Oh, I was wondering how you like teaching." The words taste funny coming out, but there's no way I can ask her out. She is Morgan's friend, a teacher at Elli's school, and much younger than me by the looks of it. The spark will fade, and I don't need the drama that would cause.

CHAPTER TWO

Reese

"I LOVE IT," I say, smiling. "It's all I've ever wanted to be. What about you?"

"I can't imagine a life where I didn't work on cars. I've never been able to be idle long, and working with my hands kept me out of trouble. Brant's like a brother to me, and his shop feels like home."

We share an awkward smile. I'm not sure what else to say. Daniel is attractive for an older man. He has to be almost ten years older than me. Brant's older than Morgan, and Daniel seems to be around his age. His rich brown eyes remind me of my favorite chocolates.

He winks. "I'm going to go check on Elli. I'm sure we will see each other again soon."

I nod. "I think that's a safe bet," I say, pointing to Brant and Morgan. I watch as Daniel walks away. That man sure has a fine backside in a pair of dress pants. Phew!

"You okay?" Morgan bumps my arm, startling me out of my thoughts. "You look like you just tasted chocolate for the first time."

I tuck a loose strand of hair behind my ear. "Yeah," I sigh. "I'm just daydreaming. You look so happy, and I'm so thrilled for you!" I lean in and give her a hug. Morgan has been my co-teacher since I graduated two years ago. I look up to her; at twenty-nine, she has been through more than any woman should. She's found happiness again after her first husband passed unexpectedly, and it gives me hope that love is really out there.

She smiles and glances across the room at Brant. Her eyes sparkle and she sighs deeply. "I'm so blessed to have fallen in love with two amazing men."

I take a sip of my sparkling wine and glance around. Daniel is in the living room kneeling down listening to Liam talk about something. Try as I might, I can't take my eyes off of him.

"Ah," Morgan says softly. "I see you've met Daniel?"

"Hmm? Oh, yes." I turn my attention back to her, ignoring the urge to watch him. "Elli had the wiggles during the ceremony, so I sat by her to help keep her still. We were chatting when Daniel came back inside."

Morgan looks around the room, spotting Elli and smiling. "She's a sweetheart. A never-ending ball of energy, that one," Morgan says. "She keeps Daniel and Heather on their toes."

Taking another sip of my drink, I smile. "Where is Heather?" I ask.

"Oh, I imagine she is enjoying her weekend. Daniel and Heather rotate weeks during the school year." Morgan sighs. "I can't imagine going a full week without seeing Liam. I think my heart would break. It's part of why we aren't taking a long honeymoon." She lifts her lips in a half smile. "Thank goodness Brant understands. He didn't want to leave Liam either." She chuckles. "I got lucky."

"You deserve it," I say honestly. "Well, I'm going to head out." I set the cup on the tray Susan designated for dirty dishes. "I've got some things to do before the new week starts. Especially since I'll be missing my favorite co-teacher."

I give Morgan a hug. "Enjoy your week off."

I wave goodbye to Susan and Sam, who are deep in conversation with another teacher, and head outside. Once I'm in my car, my head falls to the steering wheel. Weddings always make me long for a special someone of my own. I'm only twenty-four, but I feel the pressure to find someone and settle down. Especially when Mom reminds me she was already married at my age.

My phone rings and I dig through my purse. Pulling out the phone, I swipe to answer.

"Hey, Mom," I say, groaning internally. Perfect timing.

"Hi, dear. How was the wedding?" Mom's chipper voice floats through the line and lands heavily on my nerves.

"It was beautiful. Brant and Morgan look very happy." I settle back into the seat, resigned to finishing the conversation before I'm able to drive away. Talking to her can sometimes take all my focus.

"That's wonderful, honey. Listen, Mrs. Weston down the road said her son is coming home for the summer. Something about being in between jobs. I was thinking—"

I cut her off. "I'll be working this summer, Mom. Besides, I'm seeing someone." The lie rolls off my tongue, and I cringe. I can't do any more of her surprise set-ups, though.

"You are? That's wonderful, dear. Why didn't you tell me?" My mother's excitement is palpable. I think she's been more focused on my life plan than I have. She's always encouraged me to do my best, and is disappointed when she feels I haven't measured up. When her best friend's daughter got married last summer, it really amped up the pressure for me to find a "suitable" man to marry. Though I'm beginning to wonder if we have the same idea of what that means.

"It's new. Listen, Mom, I have to run. I'm going to be late for my date." Another lie. Guilt gnaws at me. I don't know why, even at my age, I still feel like I have to earn my mother's love.

"Oh goodness, I'll let you go. Go snag your man!" She chuckles. "Talk soon."

"Bye, Mom." The line falls dead, and I stare at my phone. She didn't even say I love you. I shouldn't be disappointed, but I am.

Putting the car in drive, I vow to download those dating apps today and secure a date. Maybe if I find someone quickly, the guilt about lying to my mom won't eat me alive.

At twenty-four; I've been out of school and teaching for two years—I'm ready to move into the next phase of my life. I've got a plan, including a ring and babies, but I'm hardly an old maid, contrary to my mother's delusion. My parents had me late, and mom is more than ready to be a grammy. I want a family too, but I feel like an animal at auction when she tries to marry me off to her friend's sons.

True to my guilt, I downloaded several dating apps last week. I decided to give them a go one at a time to avoid being over-whelmed by too many choices.

It didn't take long for me to be matched to a few guys in the area. When I matched with Martin on the Meet Your Match app, I was thrilled. He's nice enough looking—or at least he is in his profile pic. His bio says he enjoys reading, long walks, and golf. Perfectly respectable.

We've been texting all week, and though he's been a little short in his messages, he's been polite enough. Maybe he just doesn't like to text. He's twenty-six, only slightly older than me. He's checked all the boxes on my list, which is why, when he asked me out, I said yes.

He suggested meeting today for brunch, and I agreed. It seemed to be less pressure than a fancy dinner. Besides, we don't have many places in Piney Brook that would qualify as high class.

Groaning, I flop back onto my bed. What does one wear to a brunch date? It sounded so simple when I agreed. Now I'm not so sure.

Pushing up from my bed, I step back into my small walk-in closet. Pants and a blouse? A dress? Settling on a soft mint green dress I picked up last week, I smile. The long-sleeved dress feels like heaven when I slide it over my head. The peekaboo lace at the waste makes my usually curvy middle look tucked in. Perfect.

I run to the bathroom and finish applying my makeup. Nothing fancy, it's a day date, but a bit of shadow and gloss. I pull my hair into a low side pony and take a moment to examine my reflection. Not terrible. I can't do anything about all this red hair, but I've learned to compliment it.

I slide on my nude ankle boots and grab my purse. At this rate, I'll be lucky to be fashionably late. The restaurant is close to my apartment, so I walk the few blocks rather than drive. That's one good thing about living in an apartment right behind the main strip of town; everything is fairly close.

I step inside the quaint little diner and spot Martin sitting alone, checking his watch. I make my way to the table and smile. "So sorry," I say, pulling out my chair and sitting down. "I had a hard time deciding what to wear."

Martin stands. "I would've gotten your chair for you," he says. "I didn't see you come in. Sorry."

"It's okay," I say. "I was late. Besides, I'm used to pulling out my own chairs." I wink to let him know I'm joking. He doesn't even smile. Hmm.

"Well," he says, sitting back down. "I'm glad you made it. I was starting to wonder if I'd been stood up."

"Nope," I say, picking up my menu. "Just running behind. I'm usually pretty punctual." Hopefully he warms up when we get some food. I smile when I see the server coming to take our order.

"Welcome to Piney Brook Beats and Eats. I'm Gabby—I'll be your server today," the teen says. May I get you some coffee or juice?"

"I'll take a coffee, black. Also, a glass of water with extra ice," Martin says.

For someone who said he pulls out chairs, he certainly doesn't let ladies order first. Raising an eyebrow, I wait for him to at least say please.

Nothing.

Shaking my head, I look at Gabby. "I'll have an orange juice, please. Biggest glass you've got."

"Sure thing, Ms. Reese," Gabby says, smiling. "I'll be right back with that."

"She should have offered me coffee while I was waiting," Martin mumbles after she is away from the table.

"Excuse me?" I ask. "I'm not sure I heard that." He can't possibly be upset that she didn't bring him coffee yet. He'd only been waiting a few minutes when I arrived, and clearly they're busy. Every other table in the rustic diner is full.

"I just said service could have been faster." He shrugs. "What do they have to eat that's worth trying?"

I'm stunned silent, and I'm not sure that's ever happened to me before. I know Martin lives in the big city just a ways away from here, but surely he doesn't think that small town restaurants have nothing to offer. Since living in Piney Brook, I have fallen in love with the small town's charm.

"Everything here is good," I say with conviction. "In fact, I bet it tastes better than any chain restaurant where you live."

"Hmm," he says, eyeing the menu.

"Here we are," Gabby says, approaching the table. "Orange juice, black coffee and a water with extra ice. Have y'all decided what you're going to have?"

"I suppose I'll try the pancake platter," Martin says, handing over the menu. He doesn't even look at poor Gabby. He picks up his coffee and inhales like he's searching for hints of poison. Geez.

"You know what, Gabby," I say. "I'm not really all that hungry this morning. In fact, I think I'm not feeling so well."

"Oh, I'm sorry, Ms. Reese. Do you want some toast?"

"No thanks, Gabby," I say kindly. "Martin, I'm sorry. I'm afraid I'm going to need to leave now."

"What?" he sputters. "But we haven't even eaten."

"Yes, well," I say, standing from my chair. "I'm suddenly feeling unwell. You understand, don't you?" I dig in my purse and find my wallet. I pull out a ten-dollar bill and toss it on the table.

"Not really; you were fine a minute ago." He looks incredulous. "So you show up late and leave early? I hope you know I will not drive to this god-forsaken town to see you again."

"That's fine, Martin," I say. "I had hoped you'd lose my number, anyway. I'd rather not date someone who can't find it in themselves to be kind to people around them."

His face contorts with anger. Gabby is already stepping away from the table when I turn and walk right out the front door.

What a waste of effort. I take a breath and release my hands. I've got marks from where my nails dug into my palm. No man is worth breaking skin for.

Reaching my front door, I let out a sigh and step inside. My stomach growls. I *am* hungry, but I was certainly not going to waste my time having a meal with Mr. Sourpuss. No thanks.

I kick off my ankle boots and grab my phone from my purse. I drop the purse onto the table and sit down. My stomach can wait. I pull up Meet Your Match, and block Martin. I also block his phone number and delete our text thread. Ugh, what a despicable man.

Now I can focus on food. I'll just have to whip something up here. I open the pantry; an empty box of toaster pastries, and a bag of rice stare back at me. Oh yeah, I forgot to pick up groceries.

Opening the fridge, I spot a container of yogurt in the back. Checking the expiration date, I let out a relieved sigh. Still good.

I tear off the top and grab a spoon. Digging in, I walk into my bedroom and head straight for the drawer of comfortable loungewear. First up, groceries, then a date with my favorite book boyfriend. Why can't these men ever appear in real life?

I change into yoga pants and a worn college t-shirt. My mom would have a fit, but I'm not dressing to impress the teenager who bags my groceries. If I've got to battle the grocery store on a Sunday afternoon, I'm doing it comfortably.

Twenty minutes later, I'm pulling into the parking lot of the only grocery store in town. It's small, but it beats driving into the city. Especially after a bad first date. Thankfully, the parking lot isn't too full, and I find a space right up front.

Grabbing a cart from the corral near the front door, I head inside, determined to gather the essentials and get out before anyone sees me. The joys of living in a small town—someone knows you everywhere you go.

"Reese, is that you?" a masculine voice calls from behind me. I groan. The last thing I want is to chat. Today calls for fried chicken, sparkling water, and a good book. Slowly, I turn around.

"Hey," I say, my fake smile dissolving as I make eye contact with the one man I really, really could have gone without bumping into today. I tuck a loose strand of hair behind my ear, and remind myself I'm not trying to impress anyone.

"Hey. I thought that was you." Daniel eyes my cart and grins. "Shopping for the essentials?"

I laugh despite feeling like I want to crawl under a rock and hide. Yoga pants and an oversized shirt seemed like such a good idea half an hour ago. "Yep," I say, gesturing to the mostly empty cart and wishing a hole would open up and swallow me.

CHAPTER THREE

Daniel

"Seems we both needed to restock. Elli eats all the good stuff when she's over."

Reese grins and tucks a strand of hair behind her ear. "Kids love their snacks," she says, still smiling.

"Well . . ." I say, letting the pause last too long.

"Well, I guess I'll see you around."

"Yeah," I agree. "See you around."

I am still smiling as Reese books it away from me. What a happy surprise bumping into her here. I hadn't expected to see her again so soon. She is just as beautiful in that old college tee and those legging things women wear as she was at the wedding last weekend.

Turning, I walk down the cereal aisle. When Elli is with her mom, I can indulge my addiction without feeling like a bad influence. I grab down the biggest box of chocolate puff cereal I can find and toss it into the cart. Breakfast, dinner, or a snack—cereal is my go-to food. One perk of being single.

I make my way to the checkout stands and find Ms. Lena's lane open. I smile my best smile. "Ms. Lena, you just get prettier and prettier every time I see you," I say as I place my items on the conveyor belt.

"Daniel, you old scoundrel," she says, smiling wide. "You know I'm twice your age, at least." She fluffs her graying hair a bit.

"Age is just a number, Ms. Lena. When are you going to give me *your* number and let me take you to dinner?" I ask, winking at the older woman.

She blushes and laughs. "You're a good man, Daniel. One of these days, a woman is going to come around and steal you from me."

I place my hand over my heart. "Steal me away? Ms. Lena, you know better than that. My Elli girl is the only woman besides you who has my heart these days."

She finishes scanning my items and shakes her head. "You'll see, Daniel. Love is going to bite you in the bum, and I'm going to laugh when it does."

I put the paper bags into my cart and finish paying for my groceries. "We'll see," I say as I walk away. I can't help thinking about the cute redhead filling her cart somewhere in the store.

Pouring a big bowl of the chocolaty cereal, I plop down on the couch, and flip through the channels. Finally, I settle on an old action flick I've seen before. No sense in getting invested in something new. The game will be on soon. I've got the DVR scheduled to record it, just in case I crash early. I've got to be at work early tomorrow since Brant will be out. He and Morgan took the week off to move her things into his house and get adjusted to being married. Not much of a honeymoon, but I get it. It's hard to take time off when Morgan and Liam have school.

I shake my head and lean back into the couch. Better him than me. Brant and Morgan are the real deal. They have one of those forever loves. I can tell just by the way they look at each other when they think no one is paying attention. At one time, I thought I'd have that kind of love. I'd hoped Heather and I could get there one day, but I learned the hard way it's just not in the cards for me. I never want to be blindsided again.

The following Monday, I still can't shake the image of Reese in casual clothes in the grocery store. I think I liked that look even more than the Emerald jumpsuit she wore to the wedding.

"Hey, man," Evan calls from across the shop. "How did it go with the redhead last week? Did you make a move?"

I wipe my hands on a towel while I watch the oil drain from the car I've got on my lift. "Seriously, Ev. Don't you have anything better to worry about? That was a week ago. I'm surprised you remember." Grabbing the new filter and plug, I duck back under the car.

"Nah," Evan calls. "I'm like an elephant—I never forget. So does that mean you didn't ask her out?"

I roll my eyes and sigh. He will not give up. "Why do you care so much?" I push the oil drip can out from under the car and move to lower the lift. "Don't you have a list of women ready to date you at the drop of a hat?"

"Ha, ha," Evan says, smiling. "You know I don't keep lists. No evidence." He winks. "So, did you ask her out or what?"

"One of these days, you're going to meet someone who wipes that smirk off your face. I just hope I'm around to see it."

"Maybe," he says. "But until then, I'm a free agent." He hands me the hose that we use to pump oil into the cars. "So . . ."

"No, I didn't."

"Oh," Evan says, his face falling. "I'm sorry, man. I've never seen you interested in someone like that before."

I shrug and check the oil level one last time before closing the hood on this one. "It's all right; I'm happy single."

Evan shoots me a look that says he doesn't believe me. "D, don't you think you should give dating a shot again?" He shakes his head. "You should have asked her out. You don't really want to be alone forever, do you? Even I want to settle down someday."

"Listen, dating Morgan's friend is a bad idea. Could you imagine if I made her mad? She'd tell Morgan, and Brant would have to hear about it." I shake my head. "No thanks."

"If you say so," Evan says, doubt clear on his face.

"Women do baffling things sometimes, trust me." Heather's friends used to be so rude anytime we got into an argument. I could always tell when she'd been talking to them about our private business. I shudder.

"Whatever you say, man." Evan shuffles back to his side of the shop and gets back to work.

The rest of the day passes in a blur of appointments and phone calls. Evan doesn't have any more time to interrogate me, and I'm glad. "I'm headed out," he calls from the sink, where he's scrubbing the oil and grime from under his nails. "I'll see you in the morning."

"Sounds good. See you tomorrow." I spend a few minutes cleaning up my tools, and turning off all the equipment before popping my head in to tell Brant I'm done for the day and heading home.

Hopping into my truck, I hit my mom's number on the screen. The in-car calling new trucks have comes in handy. Especially since our county went hands-free last year.

"There's my boy." My mom's voice rings out through the cab. "I was wondering if you'd call today. How was work?"

"Hey, Mom, work was fine." I like to call her on my way home at least once a week. I've been avoiding it, though. Mom always seems to know when something is on my mind, and I definitely don't want to discuss Reese with her. "How was your day?"

"It was fine. Janice and Fred were arguing again. We had to move their rooms just to keep the peace." She giggles. "Who knew working in a retirement home part time would be so entertaining?"

I laugh. "I'm glad you're enjoying yourself. People who live in a retirement facility spend their time arguing? That's surprising. Seems they would've grown out of that by now." I guess some people never quite grow up.

"You know how it is. Get a bunch of people in the same space for a long time, tempers are bound to flare." Mom chuckled. "Elli called me today."

"That's nice," I say, smiling. Heather and I may not have worked out, but we do a fair job at co-parenting.

"She said you met someone at Brant and Morgan's wedding."

I choke on my own spit, sending me into a coughing fit. "I met several people, Mom. We were at a wedding," I say when I finally stop coughing enough to speak. Please let her drop it. I make a mental note to talk to Elli about over sharing when I see her next.

"I see," she says softly. "So a certain teacher with red hair didn't capture your attention, then?"

I groan and rub my hand over my face. "It wouldn't matter if she did, Ma," I say. "You know I'm not looking to get married again. Besides, she's a lot younger than me, and she's Morgan's friend."

"Oh, Daniel." Mom sighs. "Don't let what happened with Heather keep you from finding true love. Look at Dad and me; we were married thirty years before he passed. You and Heather weren't right for each other, but that doesn't mean there isn't someone who would be a perfect match."

"I know, Mom. I'm just not interested in getting hurt again. Separating from Heather was the right thing to do, but it kills me to have to split my time with Elli. I don't want to do that again."

"I know," Mom says quietly. "Just promise me you won't close yourself off from love."

"I promise, Ma," I say, mostly to make her feel better. I know she just wants to see her kids happily married and settled down. She and Dad were soulmates, and it breaks her heart to think I'll miss out on that kind of love. I just don't think it's in the cards for me. She'll have to be happy that my sister found someone, even if it means she moved several states away.

"Listen, I just got home, so I'm going to let you go." I put the truck into park and lean my head against the seat.

"All right, I'll talk to you soon."

"Bye, Mom." Turning off the truck, I take a minute and think about what she said. Could I ever be ready to trust my heart to someone? Somehow I don't think so. I make a mental note to have a chat with Elli when I see her at the End of the Year Carnival at school Friday night. She can't go telling everyone that I've met someone and getting her grandma's hopes up.

Friday evening, I'm standing next to Brant while we survey the auditorium of the Piney Brook Elementary School. Big paper flowers and green strips of what I'm guessing is meant to be grass line the walls. They set tables up displaying the crafts the kids have been working on this spring. Booths with games and baked goods round out the room.

"Do you see them?" Brant asks, looking around the gymnasium.

"Not yet." Out of the corner of my eye, I catch a streak of red hair rushing by. "I think I may have just seen Reese rushing in that direction." I point to the corner where the teachers have a makeshift headquarters set up.

"There they are. Come on." Brant is already walking in that direction, his long legs eating up the space. I look around for Elli and Heather one more time before shrugging and following him. Maybe they haven't gotten here yet.

"Morgan," Brant says, spying his new bride. "You and Liam ready to play some games?" He leans in and kisses her cheek. I turn my head to give them some privacy, and my eyes catch Reese staring at the newlyweds. She must feel me looking at her. She turns, her gaze catching mine, and blushes.

"Hey there," I say, smiling. "How've you been?" I feel like a teenage boy with his first crush. What is wrong with me?

"Good, you?" she asks, not quite looking me in the eye. She fidgets with the hem of her shirt. I wonder if I make her nervous too.

"Um, good. Been busy at the shop. Brant's had his head in the clouds since he came back to work this week." I shift my weight, and look at the couple now kissing while Liam stands beside them bouncing from foot to foot. His eyes light up, and he pulls on Brant's shirt. "Elli's here!" he squeals.

Turning, I spot Heather and Elli headed this way. When they get close, I pick Elli up and swing her around. "There's my bug," I say, kissing her cheek. "I've missed you."

"Daaad," she drawls. "You just saw me last weekend."

"I know, Elli girl, but that was five whole days ago." I wink at her. "Hey, Heather. Good to see you."

"Hey, Daniel. Could I talk to you for a minute?" she asks. "Elli, why don't you go with Liam and his family while I talk to your dad, okay?"

"Okay, Mom," Elli smiles and rushes to Liam's side. Brant gestures they are going to walk around and I give him a nod. Reese seems to have slipped away when I was greeting Elli.

"All right," I say. "What's up?"

Heather lets out an enormous sigh. "I've been offered a job opportunity. A great one actually."

"Okay," I say, dread sinking into my gut. "What does that have to do with me?" I ask, starting to sweat.

"It's nothing terrible," Heather says, seeing the look of sheer panic that must be on my face. "I just got an offer to travel abroad for the summer."

"When?" I ask, my heart pounding in my chest. "When do you leave?"

"I haven't agreed just yet. I wanted to talk to you about it first." She looks at the floor and shakes her head. "The thing is, I've given it a lot of thought, and I think it would be a great opportunity for me."

"You're going to have to spell this out for me, Heather. I'm not sure I'm following."

"I'm supposed to leave on Monday. The job should wrap up by the beginning of July, but I was hoping you might want to keep Elli while I'm gone. The offer is an opportunity I probably won't get again, and one I need to take if I have any shot at making partner."

My mouth falls open. "Are you sure you want to leave our girl for that long?" I ask. "I'm sorry," I say immediately. "That was insensitive.

I'm sure you don't *want* to leave her." I rub my hands on my jeans. "Of course I'll keep Elli; that's not even a question."

"I've thought about it. She loves spending time with you, and I know she'll be taken care of. This is something I feel like I need to do." Heather sighs and looks around the packed room, her eyes not meeting mine.

"Does she know?" I ask. My eyes scan the room until they fall on Elli's bright smile.

"Not yet." Heather sighs. "I was hoping we could tell her together. Are you free for dinner after this?"

"Yeah," I say, blowing out a breath. I'm excited at the prospect of having Elli with me for a week, but I'm uncertain how she'll react to the news.

"Great." Heather smiles at me, her eyes glistening with emotion. "Thank you, Daniel."

"Let's go spend time with our girl," I say before heading off to find Elli.

CHAPTER FOUR

Reese

I'M TELLING MORGAN ABOUT the disastrous date with Martin when Brant and Daniel walk up. I swear Daniel sucked all the air from the room when he smiled at me. My fingers find the hem of my shirt. A nervous habit I picked up as a kid trying to be on my best behavior so I didn't embarrass my mom—again.

I wonder how soft Daniel's hair would be if I reached out and touched it. My fingers itch to find out. I imagine running my fingers through the longer brown waves on the top, and smoothing down the shorter sides and back.

"Elli's here!" Liam yells, breaking the spell. Daniel turns and looks for his little girl, his whole body softening with her approach. He seems to be a great dad; exactly what I hope my future husband will be like with our kids. He swoops her up and starts spinning her in the air. Elli giggles and holds his neck tight. Her mom—Heather, I think her name was—looks just like her. She's smiling at their antics, and suddenly I feel very out of place.

Quietly, I slip away and head to the musical chairs area. The prizes are pies this year, and the game seems to be a big hit. Apparently everyone likes pie.

I can't stop myself from looking over to where Heather and Daniel are deep in conversation. He looks upset, his face stricken with panic. I wonder what's happening there.

"Hey, Reese," Morgan calls. "We're going out to eat after this—want to join us?"

"Oh, I couldn't possibly intrude." I make my way to where they are standing behind the kids, watching them throw rings at bottles hoping to win a prize.

"Nonsense," Brant says, squeezing Morgan's hand. "You're welcome to join us."

"I don't think so," I say, smiling. My eyes wander to where Daniel and Heather are still talking. "It's been a long day, and I'm about ready to crash. Thanks anyway."

"If you change your mind, you're always welcome," Brant says, smiling.

"I wonder what that's all about?" Morgan asks quietly, following my eyes.

"My mom's going away for a while," Elli says, taking Liam's hand and rushing to the face-painting booth.

"What?" Morgan and I ask rushing to keep up with them.

"Oh, yeah," Elli says, nodding her head. "Mom doesn't know I heard her talking to Grandma about it, but she needs to go work in Canada for a while."

Morgan and I share a look. "How do you feel about that?" Morgan asks gently.

"Fine." Elli shrugs her little shoulders. "I heard Mom say that I'll be staying at Daddy's. I like staying with Daddy. It'll be fun." She steps up, plops in the open seat and points to a butterfly she'd like painted on her face.

Brant is watching as Daniel and Heather make their way to the booth. I feel my cheeks heat. I really shouldn't have been a part of this conversation.

When Daniel and Heather finally step close enough to hear, Brant quietly lets them know that Elli already knows. Heather looks worried. Daniel reaches over and squeezes her hand. Jealousy flashes through me, white hot. For a moment, time stands still. I imagine his warm hand squeezing mine; tingles light the nerves on the palm of my hand. I rub it nervously on my pants, willing myself to snap out of it. It's not like me to feel so attracted to someone.

"I'm going to head home," I blurt, my sudden declaration interrupting the conversation.

"What? No," Morgan says. "I really wanted you to go to dinner with us. We were just inviting Daniel, Heather, and Elli to come too." Morgan's head tilts to one side, noticing my flushed face and shaking hands. "Are you okay?"

"Yeah, I'm just tired and ready for a hot shower. I've got a date tomorrow, and I don't want to be exhausted." I smile. "It was nice to meet you, Heather. Good luck on your trip. Daniel," I say, nodding in his direction. He's frowning a bit. I wonder if he's not as thrilled about the new arrangement as Elli is.

"You too," Heather says, placing her hand on Elli's shoulder.

After telling Liam and Elli goodbye, I turn and dash towards the makeshift teachers' area to grab my things.

Tomorrow, I'm meeting a man named Ethan in Beaver Falls, the next town over, at the bowling alley. I'm not a great bowler, but he is in a league. So, I imagine if we date, I'll be spending a lot of time there. May as well give it my best shot.

The sound of pins crashing against the soft pinewood floors ring through my ears the moment I step into the bowling alley. A weird combination of stale beer and greasy food seems to seep into my skin. I shudder and glance at my watch. Seven on the dot. Hmm.

Ethan said he would meet me here. I look around, comparing every guy to the picture I remember from the dating app. I blow out a deep breath, my eyes catching on a group of guys hanging around one of the far lanes. When a tall blond waves his hand at me, I blink.

No way.

The blond comes jogging forward. "Hey, you're Reese, right?" He leans in and gives me a hug. "I'm glad you could come."

My mouth opens and closes. "Um, me too," I manage.

"C'mon, the guys are over here." He grabs my hand and pulls me toward the group I spotted him with. Confusion makes my steps falter, and he stops. "What's wrong?"

"I'm sorry," I say, trying to figure out what is happening. "Are we bowling with them?"

He looks at me, one eyebrow cocked and a smirk on his face. "Nah, it's our bowling league practice night. I thought you'd want to see me in action." He waggles his eyebrows suggestively and grins.

"Of course," I say, pasting on a bright smile. "Lead the way."

"That a girl," he says before resuming his quick pace. "Hey, guys, this is Reese, my date." The guys all hoot and give him high fives.

"Uh, hi," I say, not bothering to correct him. I mean, I thought it was a date ... It is a date, right? Kind of. Oh, who am I kidding? He invited me to watch him and his friends bowl. Ugh.

After a few minutes, everyone settles down, and the game starts back up. Ethan stands beside me, his arm around me and his hand on my shoulder. I would like to shake it off, but I don't move—I don't want to cause a scene. Besides, public displays of affection are good, right? I roll my eyes at myself. What the heck is happening here?

When it's his turn to bowl, I take a seat and plaster a grin on my face. Inside, I cringe. Is this what dating has become? Guys showing off in front of their friends?

Ethan bowls a strike, and turns and winks at me. Making his way back to the seating area, he high fives his friends, who are seated around the small table waiting for their turn.

"Listen, Reese," Ethan says, sitting beside me and squeezing my shoulder. "We're about done here—I was thinking we could head back to my place and get to know each other."

The suggestive tone behind his invitation makes me cringe. I feel the heat fill my cheeks. He can't be serious, right?

"Ooohhh, you dog!" Brenden, if I remember his name right, says, fist-bumping him. He turns and yells out, "Ethan's taking Reese back to his place." All the guys whoop and make inappropriate remarks.

Embarrassment gives way to anger. "I don't think so," I say, gritting my teeth so hard I'm sure I'll have a headache in the morning.

"C'mon, babe," Ethan says, laughing. "I mean, we met on a dating app, right? You do realize those are for hookups."

"Hookups?" I repeat lamely. "Hookups. Well, Ethan, I don't do hookups. Seems we've had a miscommunication." I stand, grabbing my purse. "The night's young though, I'm sure you can find another 'hookup' without even trying."

I spin on my heel and head for the carpeted walkway that leads to the exit. A hand grabs my arm. "Wait a minute." His face is flushed.

Whether from shame or anger, I don't know. "You can't just leave. What the heck, Reese?"

"I never agreed to a hookup. I agreed to a date. Obviously, I misunderstood, but this isn't what I'm looking for."

"You're kidding right? Everyone knows dating apps are not for finding your soulmate. We're only twenty-four!" The muscle in his jaw quivers. "I can't believe I wasted my time on you."

"Same," I say hotly. I yank my arm free and stomp out the door. By the time I make it into my car and lock the door, I'm shaking from head to toe. I take a slow, deep breath and let it out. Inhale through the nose, blow out the candles. It's a trick my second-grade teacher taught me when I would get too nervous to speak in class.

Finally feeling a little more settled, I start my car and hit the voice button. "Call Anne," I say, needing to vent to my only other single friend in Piney Brook. After just two rings, Anne's sweet voice comes over the line.

"Reese, you okay? I thought you had a date."

"I did too. Turns out, he thought I'd want to sit around and watch him and his friends bowl, then be a quick hookup later." A single tear makes its way down my cheek. "I can't believe this."

"Oh my." Anne sounds as bewildered as I feel. "Why don't you come over here? I've got leftover pizza in the fridge, and half a bottle of wine with our name on it."

"Thanks, I'll be there in a few minutes." I hit the button to end the call, and head for Anne's apartment, relieved not to be going home to fume alone.

Twenty minutes later, I'm knocking on her door.

"Hey," Anne says, opening the door with her cat in her arms. "How are you?"

I step in and give the cat, Shelby, a scratch on the head, earning a purr. "Better now that I'm here. Thanks for this." I gesture to the table where a box of cold pizza and two wine glasses sit.

"No problem," she says, smiling. "I would have heard about the date at your appointment on Monday anyway—we've just sped up the process." Anne closes the door and puts Shelby, her cat, back on the floor.

"Here," she says, handing me a plate after she's washed her hands. "Load up and we'll head to the living room, turn on some reality TV, and you can tell me all about Mr. Hookup."

I snort. "Not much to tell, but sure." I stack three pieces of pizza onto my plate and pour a healthy glass of wine.

Settling into her super soft couch, I take a sip of the wine and set the glass on the coffee table. Anne's a hairstylist at the only salon in town, and her style—from her clothes to her furniture—is cozy and warm, thrift-store sheik.

"Okay," Anne says, turning the television on. "Spill. Was he at least better looking than Mr. Sourpuss?"

I laugh at the reminder of Martin, the brunch date gone bad, and shake my head. "I really don't understand what I'm doing wrong," I say between bites of pizza. "I'm twenty-four—that's plenty old enough to be looking for a serious relationship, right?"

Anne nods her head in agreement and motions for me to continue.

"Yeah, well, Mr. Hookup didn't seem to think so."

Anne wipes her face with a napkin and grins. "Sounds like he definitely isn't 'the one' for you," she says, making finger quotes. "Did you feel any sparks before he showed his creepy side at least?"

I let out a loud maniacal laugh. "Uh no. He put his hand on my shoulder, and I wanted to shake it off. The guy gave me the creeps."

"I see," she says, her brows drawing in. "Can I ask you something?"

"Sure." I shrug. "Ask away."

"When's the last time you felt a spark with someone?" Anne takes a sip of her wine and waits patiently for me to answer her.

Immediately, Daniel pops into my mind. That's crazy, though. Meeting someone at a wedding doesn't count. Of course you feel sparks—it's a wedding. Love is in the air and all that. And the few times after that . . . Well, those are just leftovers. From the wedding. Like the top layer of the cake the bride and groom save for their first anniversary.

"Him," Anne says, pointing her finger at my face. "Tell me about whoever it is you were thinking about just now."

I shake my head and take another bite of pizza. "It's no one. Doesn't even count," I say when I finish chewing.

"Uh-uh." She grins. "Tell me anyway."

I sigh and roll my eyes. "I'm telling you it doesn't count. I met him at my co-teachers wedding. He's a friend of her new husband, and much older than me. He's divorced and has an eight-year-old daughter, for goodness sake."

"Mmhmm, and why wouldn't that count?" she asks, her eyebrow rising into her bangs.

"Because he can't be 'the one' when he's older than me and already has a kid. That's not in the plan. Remember the plan?" I ask incredulously.

"Plans change," she says simply. "I'd totally date an older hottie!"

I shove her arm playfully. "Be serious." I laugh. "My parents would have a fit if I brought home an older man, especially a single father."

"Seems to me you're an adult. I'm just saying, if I felt a spark, I'd totally see where it went." Anne scoots further back into the couch, letting Shelby climb up and cuddle into her side.

"Mmhmm, well, I'll remember that," I say, tipping my glass of wine to my mouth and finishing the glass. "Can we watch a stupid movie and forget about guys and dating, please?"

She tosses me the remote. "You choose. I'll go get us waters and clean up the pizza."

Scrolling through the options, I settle on Princess Bride—a classic—and snuggle into the couch.

By Wednesday morning, I'm just about over my irritation with Ethan. He tried texting me and apologizing several times over the last few days. I finally just blocked his number and deleted Meet Your Match. No more disaster dates for a while.

I'll just focus on my job. I'm standing in a classroom full of four- and five-year-olds with paint on my favorite shirt—the joys of leading arts and crafts.

"Okay, kiddos," I say, clapping my hands to get their attention. "Take Mrs. Anderson your papers and then line up by the sink for hand-washing time."

Preschool is my favorite age group, and this class is my favorite so far. I've only been teaching for two years, so I don't have much to compare them to, but they've been a fun group of kids. Even if they do ruin my favorite clothes.

The kids all hand Morgan their papers, and line up at the two sinks we have in the room for just this purpose. "I can't believe today's the last day of school," Morgan says quietly.

"Me either," I say, wiping the table down. "It feels like the school year just started."

"I'm looking forward to the summer," Morgan says, smiling. "Liam and Elli are going to have a ball playing together, and I will get some down time. It's the first time in years I haven't had to worry about making those paychecks last all summer."

I grin. "Well, when I'm not tutoring anyone, I'd love to hang out with you guys."

"That sounds great! I didn't know you were tutoring this summer."

"Yep," I say, grabbing the snack bags from the counter and passing them out. "I placed an ad in the paper, and I've got a sign up at the library. Samantha said the study room is pretty empty during the summer, so she's sure I can reserve it for sessions."

Morgan nods her head before taking over snack time and the next lesson of the day. Co-teaching is great. This year, we split tasks so that we could each have time to work one on one with kids who needed more help. Plus, it gives us a break from having to be the person in charge all day.

Since it's the last day of school, there's no individual instruction, and we've been packing up our classroom bit by bit. It's sad. I'm not sure how we are already at the end of the year. We spend nine months filling the classroom with art, learning, and joy, only to pack it all up at the end.

Finally, the bell rings as I'm placing the last of the manipulative supplies in the storage tote where they'll stay until the end of summer. Snapping the lid shut, I go stand at the door and wait to lead them out to the pick up and bus areas for the last time.

CHAPTER FIVE

Daniel

IT'S WEDNESDAY, ELLI'S LAST day of school. I left work early today to pick her up, even though Morgan said she could take her to their house after school again. She's been amazing, watching Elli after school each day, but there are some things I just need to be there for. The last day of school is one of them. Plus, I have a surprise for my girl.

I sign in at the office, and pick up my parent badge.

"Mrs. Harold's classroom is down the hall to the right, room 201."

"Thanks, Mrs. Patterson," I say, grinning. Of course I remember where Elli's classroom is. Heather and I have had to come in several times this year for parent-teacher meetings. Elli has struggled a bit in second grade. The teacher suspects she isn't applying herself, but I worry there might be more going on. School was never easy for me, either.

Standing in front of the wooden door, I take a peek through the small pane of glass and see my girl packing up her desk, throwing things in her backpack haphazardly. That'll be fun to go through later.

I knock before stepping into the room. "Mrs. Harold," I say, nodding. "I hope you don't mind. I came to get Elli."

"Hi, Mr. Stevens." Mrs. Harold makes her way down the row of desks and comes to stand by me at the front of the room. "Actually, if you could stay behind for a few minutes, I'd like to discuss something with you."

Dread pools in the bottom of my stomach. I catch Elli's face drop as her eyes ping-pong from me to the teacher. I send her a reassuring smile. Whatever it is, we'll get through it. I know Elli has been feeling the pressure this year. School went from relatively easy for her to becoming more difficult as the school year pressed on.

"Sure thing." I paste on a huge smile and head over to help Elli finish packing up her things before sending her down the hall to Morgan's classroom. Thankful yet again that Morgan has come into our lives.

"Thanks for waiting, Mr. Stevens." Mrs. Harold sits behind her desk and motions for me to take a seat across from her.

"No problem," I say, sliding into the tiny seat. What is the weight limit on these things? "How can I help you?"

"Well," she sighs. "As you know, Elli has struggled a bit in school this year."

I nod and wait for her to continue, limiting my movement in case the legs on this tiny chair decide to give out.

"I'm recommending that she either attends summer school or that you hire a private tutor. She'll need to continue working on her reading and math facts for third grade." She smiles softly. "Elli is a good kid. She is bright and loves to learn, but she struggles with memorizing math facts, and her reading fluency isn't where I'd like to see it."

I grimace. Seems Elli girl takes after me in the school depart-ment. "I understand." Boy do I ever understand. "Is there anything we can do at home? I really don't want to send her to summer school."

Mrs. Harold shakes her head. "In third grade, the kids will be expected to recall math facts quickly. She'll also be expected to read fluently and comprehend what she has read at a much faster pace." She pauses, taking a moment to gather her thoughts. "I really feel she needs something more focused. One-on-one tutoring would be my first suggestion, but I understand that is an added expense and time commitment. With her mother out of the state, it might be easier for her to attend summer school."

"I see. Money and time aren't an issue." I take a breath. "What if there is something more going on than just needing more practice?" I hesitate to ask, but I've been doing some reading and wonder if she may have a learning disability. While I'd never been formally tested, I suspect I may have battled with dyslexia and dyscalculia myself. I don't want my girl to struggle if there is a way we can help her.

"Well, the screening tests we give each student in second-grade, show that she is on the lower end of the normal range. She doesn't hit the markers we would expect for there to be a learning difference, but it's possible."

I place my head in my hands. I worry, not for the first time, that having a split home is working against her. Heather and I try, but there are always a few things that slip through the cracks.

"Mr. Stevens," Mrs. Harold's voice pulls me out of my thoughts. "I suggest you try tutoring this summer—one on one would be best. If she is still having a hard time, then you can request she have additional testing done to see if she has any underlying issues we could address."

I take a deep breath and let it out slowly. "I'll look into the tutor option. I appreciate your concern, and your advice."

"Summer school starts in two weeks, so you have some time to find someone to tutor her. If you don't, I would suggest summer school as a backup option." Mrs. Harold shuffles some papers on her desk, and I take that as my cue to leave.

"Thanks," I say, getting to my feet. "I'll take care of it. Have a great summer, Mrs. Harold."

"You too." She stands and shakes my hand. "It's been a joy having Elli in my class, Mr. Stevens."

"Thanks." Now, to go break the news to Elli.

I find her sitting in Morgan's pre-k classroom with containers of markers and pencils on the table in front of her. "Hey, Elli girl, what are you doing?" I ask, swooping her up and swinging her around. Her giggles fill the room, and some of the weight I carried from Mrs. Harold's classroom lifts. I hug her to me and soak up her sweetness.

"I'm helping pack up the classroom," she says proudly. "Ms. Morgan asked me to put all the pencils in one box and the markers in the other one."

I set her back on her feet. "I see," I say seriously. "That's a big job. Are you almost done?"

"Almost," she says, sitting back at the tiny table and getting to work.

I ruffle her hair and leave her to it. "Morgan, can I talk to you for a second?"

"Sure, what's up?" Morgan sets the papers she was taking off the bulletin board on her desk and gives me her full attention.

"Mrs. Harold suggested summer tutoring for Elli to help her stay on track for third grade. Would you be able to tutor her while she's with you?"

Morgan smiles and shoots a glance at Elli. "Well . . ." She pauses. "I would prefer not to—I think Elli sees me more as a friendly adult than a teacher. She would probably respond better in an environment that is set up for tutoring. Plus, having Liam running around might be too much of a distraction."

My shoulders sag. "Yeah, I get it. I just don't know how I'll get her to tutoring and juggle everything. I struggled in school, and I hate that she seems to be having the same issues."

"Who needs tutoring?" Reese's rich voice cuts through the room, surprising me. Since she hadn't been in the room when I came in, I assumed she'd already gone for the day. I know teachers are working the rest of the week submitting final grades and packing up classrooms. I took the rest of the week off to hang out with Elli and Liam for Morgan. It's the least I could do since Morgan offered to keep Elli for me while I work this summer.

"Elli could use some extra help to avoid the summer slide," Morgan says, winking at me. What the heck is that about?

"Oh, I'd be happy to tutor her." Reese smiles, and the breath leaves my lungs. I've got to get it together. She is young, and I'm not interested. Right?

"Oh, I don't know . . ." I trail off. I can't for the life of me think of a single valid reason Reese shouldn't be the one to tutor Elli. That she makes me feel things I'd rather not isn't something I'm up for sharing.

"No, that's perfect!" Morgan grins. "I can bring her to you at the library, and Liam and I can look at books while she does her tutoring. Unless you have space at the end of the day, then I can drop her off and Daniel can pick her up after work." She claps her hands together and looks excitedly between Reese and me.

"The end of the day is perfect. I haven't filled that slot. I have 4 to 5:00 on Tuesdays and Thursdays open. What do you think, Daniel? I'm charging thirty-five dollars a session." Reese looks at me expectantly, a smile tugging on her full lips.

"Um, sure. Sounds good," I grunt out. It sounds like a disaster waiting to happen, but I'll do anything for my Elli girl.

"Great, it's settled!" Reese grins and walks over to the table where Elli is working on the last bit of sorting. "Looks like you and I will get to spend some time together this summer."

Elli looks up and smiles. "Yay! What are we going to do?"

"We're going to make sure you don't forget what you've learned this year and get you ready for third grade." Reese grins from ear to ear like it's the best adventure ever.

"Oh," Elli's face falls. "I don't want to do more school." She pouts and gives me the biggest set of puppy dog eyes she can muster.

"It'll be fun. Nothing like regular school." Reese holds out her pinky. "Pinky promise."

Elli looks at her outstretched hand and raises an eyebrow. "I don't know how it isn't going to be like school, but okay." She slides her little pinky into place, and they shake on it.

"Wait and see," Reese says, winking at her.

"All right, Elli," I say, tucking my hands into my pockets. "Let's get out of here. There's a pepperoni pizza and some arcade games calling our name."

Elli jumps up and grabs her bag. "Really? We're going to Pizza and Playtime?"

"Well, we have to celebrate the end of second grade somehow, don't we?" I ask.

Elli jumps up and down. "Can we invite Liam too?"

"Well, that's up to Morgan." Elli and I turn and give Morgan our best pleading looks.

She laughs and shakes her head. "It's fine with me. I'll go grab him from after care and meet you out front."

"Yay!" Elli yells, throwing her hands in the air. "Best day ever!"

"Thanks for agreeing to tutor her," I say to Reese. "We'll see you soon, I guess."

"Let's plan to start next week." She grins at Elli. "I'm looking forward to working with you."

Elli's grin fades a bit. "Okay," she says, lacing her hand in mine. "Can we go now, Daddy?"

"Have fun celebrating," Reese calls as Elli drags me toward the door. I give a small wave and step out into the hallway.

"Elli," I say, softly. "It's okay to need some more help. I didn't do so well in school either. Grandma had to help me every day."

"She did?" Her big brown eyes find mine. "Really?"

I nod. "Really."

"Okay," she sighs. "I guess it's okay then."

"That's my girl." I squeeze her hand in mine, and together we head for the parking lot and freedom.

CHAPTER SIX

Reese

THE NEXT FEW DAYS pass in a blur of boxes and cleaning supplies. I wipe a hand across my forehead and look around the mostly empty room. Desks are cleaned and placed in rows, and the chairs are stacked in the corners. Once-colorful walls are now barren. It's strange.

"Well, that was the last of it," Morgan says, stacking the last tote in the back corner of the room. Thankfully we will be in the same room again in the fall, so we're allowed to leave our things neatly in the corner of the room. I wish they'd let us keep everything on the walls, but that's a no go. "Just in case," Mr. Jones said.

"Thank goodness. I'm ready for summer vacation." I grin and take a long drink from my water bottle.

"Think you can wait another hour or so? Susan and I were going to grab a late lunch down at Beats and Eats."

"Absolutely," I say, grinning. "I owe Gabby, anyway. Hopefully Martin didn't give her too bad of a time when I walked out on our date." I cringe and Morgan laughs.

"Gabby's tough. I'm sure she handled it just fine. Plus, you know Billy and Mrs. Daisy won't let anyone cause a fuss in there."

Twenty minutes later, we are walking into Beats and Eats, laughing.

"Well, aren't y'all a sight for sore eyes," Mrs. Daisy says, grabbing three menus. "I been wondering when y'all would make it in."

"Hey, Mrs. Daisy," Susan says, grinning. "We had to pack up our classrooms this week, or don't you remember back to when you were teaching right alongside us?"

Mrs. Daisy shakes her head, her graying bun wobbling on the top of her head. "Now, those were the days." She laughs and turns to lead us to a booth in the back. "Best seat in the house," she says, placing the menus on the corner of the table. "Gabby'll be over in a jiffy to get your orders."

I slide into the booth and grab a menu. "I didn't know Mrs. Daisy used to be a teacher."

"Oh, yeah. She was the toughest cookie around." Susan laughs. "She retired the year Morgan came to work."

Once we are all settled at the table, Gabby comes over to get our order. I cringe. "Sorry about last time," I say as I hand her back the menu. "That guy was a piece of work."

Gabby grins. "Are you kidding? That was the best day ever! After you left, I asked if he still wanted me to put in the order. He lost it and started screaming about how horrible small towns are and how dumb I was. Billy came out from the kitchen, grabbed that stuck-up creep by the collar and marched him out the door." She laughs. "I've never seen anyone look like a fish out of water before, but he was flopping around and his mouth was gaping like a landed trout."

I chuckle. "I'm glad someone got some joy out of that disaster."

"Oh, we all had a good laugh," Gabby says. "I'll be right back with your drinks."

"All right," Susan says as Gabby walks away. "Spill it. What happened?"

I relay the entire story, starting with the brunch date and ending with Ethan and the bowling hookup that never was. Our food comes while I'm still spilling the tea, as it were, but I don't stop. It feels good to get it all off my chest.

"Wow," Susan says, taking a bite of her sandwich. "You've had some awful dates lately."

"You're telling me." I pop a fry into my mouth and chew. "If it weren't for bad luck, I'd have no luck at all."

"Sounds to me like you need to let loose a little. Go outside your comfort zone." Susan raises a brow in my direction.

"How much more out of my comfort zone can I get? I downloaded dating apps, for goodness sake." I shake my head and wipe my hands on my napkin. "Any more out of my comfort zone, and I'd be going on dates my mom sets up. Which, by the way, is a real possibility if I can't produce a boyfriend when I see her next week."

Morgan chokes on her drink, and water sprays from her mouth covering her salad. "I'm so sorry," she gasps, grabbing for a napkin. "You're not serious though, right?"

"Serious as a heart attack," I say, handing her more napkins from my side of the table. "My mom is all about appearances. Her best friend's daughter got married last summer, and it just won't do that I'm not at least headed in that direction." I shrug. "I love my mom, and I do want to be married, but I feel so much pressure sometimes, that I'm scared I'll choose someone just to make her happy and end up miserable."

"You're what, twenty-four?" Susan asks. "That is still plenty young these days. Shoot, when I got married, I was still in college. I thought my mom and dad were going to have a fit. They thought we would do a long engagement and get married after graduation." She sighs, a far-off look in her eye. "We just couldn't wait. We were so in love and ready to start the next phase of our lives."

Morgan smiles. "Love comes when it's time. Not a minute before, and usually not when you're looking for it."

I sigh. "I know."

"So," Susan says pointedly. "Out of your comfort zone."

I roll my eyes. A bad habit I've tried to break, but it sneaks back in every now and again. "How do you suggest I do that?"

"Stop going for the guy you think your mom would approve of. Look for the guy who makes your heart race and goosebumps skitter across your skin," she says, waving a fry in my direction.

I feel the heat rise to my face before I can stop it.

"Ah," she says knowingly, and smirks at Morgan. "Looks like she may have someone in mind."

"Nope," I squeak. "No, I'm just embarrassed." My face flames with the lie. Daniel immediately came to mind, but he's too old. A father already. Certainly not someone I could fall in love with. What would we even have in common?

"Mhmm," Susan says, smiling. "Whatever you need to tell yourself, honey. But if I were you, I'd explore that."

Monday morning, I'm in the car chugging coffee like the caffeine will shield me from the inquisition coming my way. Mom's been calling me all weekend begging me to come spend a few days at home now that I'm on summer break. Thankfully, I have tutoring to prepare for, so I told her that wasn't a possibility. She settled for a day visit today.

The hour-long drive passes way too quickly, and I'm parked in their driveway beside a sleek two-door sports car I don't recognize. I consider putting the car in reverse and saying I woke up sick . . . when the front door swings open and my mom stands in the doorway grinning from ear to ear.

I take a deep breath and grab my purse. Better get it over with.

Stepping out of the car, I take my time closing the door, hoping somehow that will pause whatever is causing the dread to rise up in my stomach.

"Reese, darling. You made it." My mom's voice is doing that thing where it's just a tad too high for normal speech. "I'm so glad you could come today."

"I told you I'd be here," I say, plastering on a smile. "Hi, Mom." She leans in and gives me a side hug before guiding me inside.

"Reese, there's someone I'd like you to meet."

I stifle the groan that is trying to make itself heard. Please be her new bridge partner. Please don't be a man. Please, please, please.

"Grant, this is my daughter, Reese. Reese, this is Grant, Becky Sue's nephew. He's in town for a few weeks helping his aunt with some of her investments." Mom's eyebrows rise to her hairline as though this is big news.

"Nice to meet you," Grant says, stepping forward and taking my hand. He pulls it to his mouth and places a kiss on my fingers.

"The pleasure is all mine, I'm sure," I say, fighting the urge to yank my hand back and run out the door screaming. I'm sure Grant is a fine young man. A gentleman, even, but I can say with certainty, I'm not interested in him. There is no spark, no interest, nothing. Just a man whose suit is ill fitting, and whose hands are too soft.

"Now, Reese," Mom says, looking like the cat that got the canary. "I know you expected to spend the day with me, but I'm just not feeling quite up to it. I've already told Grant I'll have to reschedule our investment meeting, but I figure, why waste the day, right? So, I want you to take Grant to the craft bazaar at the community center today. Show him what our town is all about. You don't mind, do you, dear?"

"Momma," I say, saccharine sweetness dripping off every word. "Where's Daddy? I haven't even gotten to say hello."

Her smile slips just a bit. "Oh dear, yes, well, he had to run some errands for me, which is yet another reason it's best we reschedule with Grant."

"I see." I raise an eyebrow, but let it go. What Momma wants, she gets. "I'd be happy to show Grant the craft show for you, Mother."

"Oh, good. I just knew you would." She presses her hands together in front of her. "Now you two run along. I'll have lunch ready around noon. You absolutely must stay for lunch—both of you. I insist. It's the least I can do for the change in plans."

"Sounds wonderful," I say through the fake smile that is starting to hurt my cheeks.

"Of course, Mrs. Sunderland." Grant bends his arm at the elbow and I slide my hand into the crook as we step out the front door I just came in.

"She's pretty persistent," Grant says, smiling. "If I didn't know better, I'd think this was her plan all along."

I let out a small laugh. "If I know my mother, I'd say it's a safe bet."

"I figured, but I didn't know if you were in on it at first." Grant laughs as I spin to look at him. "I said *at first*. You've got the doting sweet southern daughter act down pat."

I stare at him, my mouth dropped open.

"Listen," he says, putting both hands up in a gesture of surrender. "I get how southern moms can be. I'm pretty sure my mom and aunt conspired with your mom to make this happen. For some reason

Aunt Becky needed me to come this week. I had to rearrange my entire schedule."

"Ah," I nod, finally feeling some of the fight leave me. "So you really understand?"

He grins. "Yep. Now, I don't want you to be disappointed, but . . ." He looks around and waves at the front window. "Your mom was watching." He laughs. "Anyway, as I was saying—I'm seeing someone."

"You are?" I ask, surprise causing the words to rise awkwardly.

"I am, and frankly it's pretty serious. My mom is hoping I'll settle down with someone closer to home and want to move back. I think this is her last ditch effort to change my mind. Even if Piney Ridge is still thirty minutes away."

I laugh out loud this time. "I see. Well, let's not stand here in my driveway. We have a date to go on." I wink before heading to the passenger side of his sports car.

He comes around and opens my door. "I can't wait."

The community center parking lot is packed. The annual summer craft bazaar is a highlight of the sleepy community. We finally find open parking near the back of the lot, and Grant backs into the space.

"You ready for this?" I ask, about to unfasten my seatbelt.

"I really don't know." He shakes his head as he watches elderly women tote baskets of fabric and ribbon towards the doors.

"At least you can cross 'craft fair' off your bad date bingo card," I say before stepping out of the low car and stretching my legs. "How do you drive around in that thing all the time?" I ask, pressing my hands into my lower back.

He shrugs. "It was my dream car, and the first thing I bought when I made junior partner at the investment firm."

I nod. "I understand dreams. I don't understand cars so tiny you have to fold yourself inside, but to each his own."

Grant meets me at the front of the car and extends his arm. I slip my hand into the crook of his elbow and we follow behind an older couple who are shuffling their way to the entrance of the building.

"Tell me, what have you scratched off your bad-date bingo card?" He smirks and raises his brow.

"You don't even want to know," I mutter. "Besides, today is about you."

He lifts his hands in surrender. "Okay, okay," he says laughing. "What about you? What do you do?"

We continue to make small talk as we head into the crowded building. Grant is a nice guy, but there's no chemistry. Thankfully, since he is dating someone else anyway. I shake my head. Meddling mothers.

After stopping by each table, and making sure every gossip in town got a look at us out on our 'date,' I'm laughing in earnest. Grant rubs his cheeks. "I didn't realize it's considered polite to grab people's faces anymore."

"Oh, come on. Didn't your grandma ever pinch your cheeks when you were a kid?" I lean in like I'm going to pinch him now.

He steps back, his hands in front of his face in defense. "Yes, she did, but she hasn't done that in years."

I shrug. "Some things never change around here."

"There you kids are," a sweet voice calls from behind us. "I just knew I'd bump into you here."

"You did?" I ask sweetly. "I wonder how? I didn't even know we would be here today, did you?" I ask Grant.

"Nope," he says, smiling. "Hi Aunt Becky, I'm assuming Reese's mom called you and told you we'd be here?" The question seems to catch her off guard.

"Well, yes. Of course, dear." She pats his already pink cheek. "She called just a bit ago and told me that Reese couldn't wait to show you around our little craft fair. People work all year to showcase their goods, you know. Crafting seems to be a lost art these days."

I smile graciously and nod along.

"Now, Aunt Becky," Grant starts.

"We really have to run. We promised my mom we'd come back for lunch." I interrupt. No sense causing a scene. Besides, she's right. For some of these people, this is the highlight of their year.

"Oh, don't let me keep you then," Becky says, patting Grant on the cheek again. "Enjoy your lunch."

Before we can respond, she has already walked away, waving at one of the ladies standing at a table with big straw hats on display.

"Shall we?" Grant asks.

CHAPTER SEVEN

Daniel

I'VE ENJOYED THE LAST few days hanging with Liam and Elli. After spending way too much money at Pizza and Playtime on Wednesday, we took a much more low key approach Thursday and Friday. I hooked up the water hose to the sprinkler, and they had a blast running through the water and splashing each other. Good old-fashioned fun.

When Mom called Friday afternoon and asked if Elli could sleep over this weekend, I was relieved. That girl is a ball of energy, and she's worn me down over the last few weeks. Still, I'm glad I get to have this time with her. It's been hard sharing custody of my girl. I always imagined the house with the picket fence; the happy family; more kids. Weekends filled with family fishing trips and running through the sprinklers. Not for the first time, I am sad for what isn't to be.

I shake it off, like Elli's favorite song. The upbeat tune has been playing on repeat since school let out on Wednesday. It's catchy, but I'm ready to listen to something else.

Elli shooed me out of Mom's house as soon as we got there Friday evening. Apparently, they had important things to do. Grandma and Elli things. I love how close Elli is with my mom. I know my dad would have enjoyed her endless energy, too.

With a quiet house, and no one to interrupt, I put on the baseball game, and start cleaning up. Tornado Elli has left barbies, lego, and, for some reason, socks all over the place. The child seems to take one sock off at a time, in different parts of the house. It's like a treasure hunt to find a matching pair of socks in the mornings. I've started trying to convince her that mismatched is the way to go.

By Sunday morning, I'm bored and missing Elli. I miss the sound of her giggles. She's only been with me full time for a couple of weeks, but she's filled every inch of my house with her big personality. I'm going to miss her when Heather is back and we are back to our usual routine.

That afternoon, I pull into my mom's gravel driveway and smile. Some things never change. The rose bushes that line the front of her house are in full bloom—big red and white flowers open and fragrant. There are two new rows of snapdragons lining the walkway. This must be what they were up to. Stepping out of the truck, I hear Elli's giggles coming from the back of the house.

I follow the sound and see Elli and Mom elbow deep in a flower bed. "Hey there," I say, cutting into their fun. "What are you two up to?"

Elli jumps up from her place on the ground and races towards me, dirt flying from her hands as she runs. "Nuh uh, Elli girl, you need to clean up before you rub dirt all over my Sunday clothes. Grandma would have my behind." I laugh as she skids to a stop in front of me.

"Hi, Daddy! Grandma is teaching me how to plant flowers today." She points to the massive mess she's made in one of the flower beds. "We are planting marigolds back here. We already did the snapdragons in the front. I picked them!"

I grin. "I loved marigolds and snapdragons when I was your age. Hey, Ma." I lean in and kiss her cheek.

"Hey yourself," Mom says, grinning. "Elli and I were just finishing up. We have two more to plant. Why don't you head inside and pour us all some lemonade? We'll be in shortly."

"You bet," I say, leaving them to it.

Stepping through the back door into my mom's kitchen is like stepping back in time. The faded teapot wallpaper has started to come apart at the seams a bit, but she won't let me replace it. She says it reminds her of Dad.

I grab three glasses from the cabinet and set them on the scarred wooden table. This table has seen countless family dinners over the years. It's the same one my sister carved my name into with the back of her earring when we were little kids. She got in so much trouble for that. I laugh and run my fingers over the etched letters.

Opening the fridge, I take out the pitcher of fresh lemonade, pour some in each glass, and set the pitcher in the middle. It's hot out there today, and I know Elli—one glass of Grandma's lemonade won't be enough.

"Straight to the bathroom and wash up," Mom says as she as Elli step through the door. "Dinner's almost ready."

"Yes, ma'am." Elli scoots past me in the kitchen, careful not to get me dirty, and races down the hallway to the bathroom.

"That girl," my mom says, washing her hands in the sink. "I think she's wearing as much dirt as she left in the flower bed." She chuckles. "I miss when you kids used to help me in the garden."

"Really?" I ask, a bit surprised. "All we did was make a mess. I swear you had to do double the work to make sure things actually grew." I laugh, remembering being covered in dirt.

"It was fun to have you and Claire working beside me, though." She smiles and pats my cheek. "Time goes by too fast these days."

"Grandma," Elli calls from the hallway. "I can't get the dirt out from under my nails."

"I'll go help her," I say.

A few minutes later, Elli's nails are clean and we are all seated at the dining table. A salad, a tray of lasagna, and breadsticks are laid out in the center.

"This smells good, Ma," I say, making myself a plate of food.

"I helped, Daddy," Elli says squirming in her seat. "I got to do the layers."

I smile at Mom. "You let her do the most important part?" I ask in mock surprise. Layering the lasagna was always Claire's job. I always tried to leave the ricotta mixture out.

"She did a great job, too," Mom says, patting Elli's hand.

I take a bite and pause. "Hmm." I finish chewing and swallow. "Excellent job, Elli girl."

The rest of the meal passes with Elli listing all of her summer plans, none of which I knew a thing about, and half of which we can't afford. She keeps me on my toes, that's for sure.

Elli and I clean up the kitchen and put away the leftovers before grabbing her things and hitting the road. Tomorrow is her first day with Morgan and Liam, and I don't want her to be cranky.

"Let's go, Elli, we're going to be late," I shout down the hall to her room for the third time this morning. Apparently, she was more tired than I thought.

"Coming!" She slides around the corner in her socked feet, one blue and one purple. "I had to pack my bag." A giant tote bag is slung over her shoulder, toys popping out of the top.

"What did you pack?" I ask, shaking my head. "You're going for the day, not moving in."

"Dad." Elli draws out my name in the way kids do when they're irritated by their parents. "You know Liam is a boy, right? He has cars and superheros. No dolls. I need my dolls." She sighs and drops the bag at her feet. "What's for breakfast?"

I grab the muffin off the counter and hand it to her. "You get a muffin. In the car. You're making me late."

"Fine," she says, taking the muffin and heading to the hallway to grab her shoes. "But you have to carry my bag. It's too heavy."

I grab the overflowing purple tote from the floor where she dropped it. Looks like Barbie is bringing her friends and all her best accessories to Liam's today. "I've got it," I call, going to the front door and holding it open for her.

"Thanks, Daddy." She throws her arms around my middle and squeezes. "Oh—my muffin." She turns and runs to the bench in the hallway where she set it down. "I almost forgot."

I'm only thirty minutes late for work this morning. Which, all things considered, I'll take. After clocking in, I pop my head into Brant's office. "Hey, boss, got a minute?"

Brant looks up from the computer. "Sure, come on in. Everything okay?"

"Yeah." I sigh, taking a seat in the chair across from his desk. "I underestimated how long it would take me to get Elli out the door this morning."

Brant laughs. "Liam is like his mom. Not a morning person, to say the least. I feel your pain."

"Ouch," I say, grinning. "She usually doesn't drag her feet on school days, but she had to pack her entire Barbie collection to take to your place this morning. Apparently super hero toys and cars aren't going to be enough to entertain her today."

Brant grins. "Well, I hope one day our house is filled with all that girlie stuff."

"Wait, are you and Morgan expecting?"

"No, not yet, but we are thinking about expanding our family. I'd love a little girl, but I know Liam has his heart set on a brother. He's even started writing letters to Santa early. Says his last wish worked, so this one should too."

I crack up. "You haven't explained that Santa doesn't bring babies?"

Brant shoots me a pointed look. "I've tried. Liam's convinced Santa granted his wish last year and made his mom and me fall in love. There's no convincing him Santa just deals in toys."

I grin. "Liam's a good kid." Standing, I make my way to the door. "I don't plan on being late anymore, but who knows? Kids."

Brant just waves me off. "No problem, man. I get it."

This is part of why I've stayed working for Brant for so long. He is a stand-up guy, and has become my best friend. He was there for me when Heather and I decided to split. Listened and never judged. He has worked with my schedule to give me the most time with Elli possible. You don't find that in every workplace.

"Daniel, nice of you to make it in today." Evan throws a towel in my direction. "I've been picking up your slack all morning."

"It's thirty minutes, kid. Don't get your undies in a bunch."

Evan chuckles and hands me the keys to the next car up. "Oil change and rotate. Shouldn't be too hard for you, grandpa."

I shake my head and grab the keys. Evan is always good for some light-hearted ribbing. He's a good guy. Young, but smart. He'll be ready to take over the shop in no time, I'm sure.

By the end of the day, my hands are covered in grease, my clothes are filthy, and I'm exhausted.

"Quitting time, guys," Brant calls from his office.

"Thank goodness," Evan says, wiping his hands on a towel. "I've got plans tonight. Don't want to be late." Evan winks and raises his eyebrows suggestively.

"The only plan you have is to get takeout and watch the game," I joke.

"Yeah, yeah." He grins. "Actually, I told my new neighbor I'd help her pick up her new couch tonight."

"New neighbor, huh?" asks Brant. "Should we make extra food this weekend?"

"It's not like that," Evan says, closing the last drawer of his toolbox. "I'm just being a good neighbor."

"So, you're not going to invite her to the cookout this weekend?" Brant crosses his arms and leans into the wall. "Because we would certainly be all right with it if you did."

"We'll see," Evan says. "I'm sure she has friends of her own, and her own life. Like I said, I'm only being neighborly and all that."

"If you say so," Brant pushes off the wall and heads to the door. "I'm headed home. I'll see you at the house when you come to pick up Elli."

I nod and head to the sink to wash up. "I'll be there shortly—just going to clean up my area and close everything up."

Thirty minutes later, I'm knocking on the door of Brant's house.

"Coming," a female voice yells.

Goosebumps erupt on my skin. I know that voice. I don't have time to school my face before the door swings open and I'm standing face to face with Red.

"Hey, Daniel," she says, stepping back. "Come on in. I think Elli is just gathering her things."

I step into the house. The scent of vanilla and cinnamon envelopes me. She smells like my favorite cookies.

Reese brushes what I'm assuming is flour from her pants. "We were just baking some cookies," she says, motioning to the bar in the kitchen.

"Is that what I smell?" I ask, grinning. "Sugar cookies?" She laughs and her face lights up. I want to see her do it again. I shake my head. She's off limits—I'd do well to remember that. Especially now, since she is Elli's tutor.

"Close," she says, smiling. "Snickerdoodle."

I groan. "My favorite."

Elli comes around the corner, toys falling from her bag as she struggles to carry her load from the playroom down the hall.

Morgan is behind her picking up the doll clothes and accessories that have escaped.

"Hey, Daniel," she says while she tucks the dropped toys into the bag. "Brant's just in the shower."

"I figured." I reach out and take Elli's overstuffed bag. "You ready, Elli girl?"

Elli grins and takes my hand. "Yep."

"Wait," Reese says, rushing to the kitchen and grabbing a plastic tub from the counter. "Elli said these were your favorite cookies, so we made you two a to-go box."

She holds the box out, and I tuck Elli's bag higher onto my arm to take them. "Thanks."

Elli pulls on my hand. "C'mon, Daddy, let's go! Mommy is supposed to call me soon!"

"Thanks again," I call out to the room as Elli pulls me toward the door. "We'll see you in the morning."

Chapter Eight

Reese

It's Tuesday, and my first day of tutoring, and I'm looking forward to it. I managed to line up four clients for Tuesdays and Thursdays throughout the summer. Making those teacher checks stretch all summer isn't an easy feat, and this will help supplement my summer income.

I check the wagon I have packed with all the supplies I'll need for the afternoon and close my trunk. I'm thankful the library study rooms are available. It's an easy location to find, and quiet enough to limit distractions. Plus, the space is free, meaning I get to keep all my profits as long as I don't exchange money on the premises.

Rolling my cart through the sliding glass doors, I grin at Samantha sitting behind the circulation desk. "Hey," I say, coming to a stop. "Thanks again for letting me use the study rooms for tutoring."

"Hey Reese, good to see you!" Samantha says. "I'm just happy to have the space being utilized over the summer. I've scheduled you in room two from now until 5:30. That's what you said, right?"

"That's perfect! My last student is being picked up then." I grin and do a little dance. "I'm so excited to branch out and work with older kids this summer. I love pre-k, but I'm looking forward to the change of pace."

Samantha nods. "I get it. I like when we move to summer scheduling at the library. More kids come in with their parents for books to read than during the school year. It's fun to engage with them."

"It's good to get out of the normal routine, I think. I better go set up," I say, pulling the cart in the direction of the study rooms. "See you later."

I stand and stretch my back. The first three sessions are done, and I'm waiting on Morgan to drop off Elli. I take out the reading cards I brought, and set them on the table. I also put out the addition game I bought to use for tutoring. Kids learn better when it seems fun.

A soft knock on the open door lets me know they're here.

"Hi, Reese," Morgan says, stepping into the small room with Elli, and Liam trailing behind her. "We made it."

"Just in time." I smile at Elli. "I was just getting the games out."

Elli's head tilts to the side, her eyes wide in surprise. "Games? I thought my dad said you're gonna be doing school with me."

"Yeah, kind of," I say, pointing to the table. "I have some games and things to make it fun, though." She's skeptical—I can see it in her eyes. "Just give it a chance."

She sighs, her little shoulders slumping. "Okay," she says, looking from me to Morgan. "I hope you're right."

Morgan leans down and gives her a quick hug. "Your dad will be here to pick you up when you're done. So, Liam and I will see you tomorrow."

Elli nods. "'Kay," she says softly. "Bye, Liam. See you tomorrow."

Morgan sits Elli's tote bag, brimming with Barbie dolls, down by the doorway.

I smile and nod, letting Morgan know I've got this.

"Bye, Elli. Have fun," Liam says before asking his mom if they can look for race car books.

I sigh and close the door.

"Let's get started," I say, smiling in what I hope is a comforting way. For some reason Elli seems nervous. "What do you want to do first? Reading or Math?"

She looks up, startled. "I can choose?"

"Of course!" I push the cards and the game closer to her. "You can always choose what we do first; sound good?"

She kicks her little legs and looks from the game to the cards. "Um," she hesitates. "I'm not really so good at either of them."

"That's okay," I say encouragingly. "We are going to have fun this summer, and see if we can't get some of that tricky stuff to stick."

She smiles and taps the math game. "Let's start with the game first."

"Perfect," I say, and get to work setting it up.

An hour later, we've played the addition game twice and gone through the reading cards. I've made a pile of the ones she has down pat, and the ones she struggles with. I also make a mental note of the math facts she has the hardest time with.

From the way Daniel said Mrs. Harold talked, Elli was really struggling. After working with her today, I'm not sure she's having as hard a time as he was led to believe. I think it comes down to confidence.

"All right," I say, grinning. "I had fun with you today. Thanks for playing with me." I put the cards into separate ziplock bags so they are ready for our session on Thursday, while Elli busies herself cleaning up the math game.

"It was better than school," Elli says, giving me a side eye. "I still don't know if it was fun, though." She sighs.

"I know it feels hard, and everything we did today was new. Give it some time, and you'll be a pro before too long." I pat her back.

She slides off the chair and opens the door. Daniel pauses, hand in the air as though he was just about to knock.

"Hey, Elli girl," he says, bending down to her level. "How'd it go today?"

She wraps her arms around his neck and squeezes. "It was okay."

He stands, still holding her, and smiles at me. "Well?"

"It went great! Elli and I played a math game and worked on her reading a bit. She is a very smart girl. I'm excited to see what fun we can get into next time."

Daniel shifts Elli to his side. "Okay," he says, sounding a bit unsure. "Is there anything we need to be doing at home?"

I shake my head. "Other than reading together every night, I think you're good for now."

A look of disbelief crosses his face. "No worksheets or flash cards?"

"Nope." I smile at Elli before looking at Daniel again. "No homework in the summer."

"Uh, okay." He gives Elli a squeeze and sets her on the ground. "Why don't you go look for a few books for us to read while I talk to Ms. Reese?"

"Okay," she says before skipping off to the children's section across the aisle.

We watch her as she makes her way around the shelves, looking at the books on display on their tops.

"Are you certain we don't need to be doing more? I really don't want her to struggle." Daniel pins me with a vulnerable stare. "I struggled. I don't want that for her."

"Honestly, she's not that behind. I think she struggles with confidence more than anything."

He sighs. "How do I help with that?"

"It takes time."

"Yeah," he says, softly. "Thanks."

I nod, unsure what else to say. He gives me a half smile and turns to join Elli in the children's section.

I watch them for a moment, debating a stack of books Elli has collected at one of the tables. He's a good father.

I'm just stuffing the wagon into my trunk when my phone buzzes in my pocket. Taking a breath, I close the trunk and grab the phone.

"Hey, Mom," I sigh.

"How was your tutoring today, dear?"

"It went great. I think these kids will be well prepared when they start school in the fall." I pause, waiting for the real reason she called.

"I was hoping you'd rearrange your schedule a bit. The Deer-fields are having a dinner party, and I'd love you to be there. It's Thursday evening, semi-formal."

"Mom, I can't do that," I say, sighing. Mom has never taken my job as seriously as I have. She's always considered it a stepping stone to my real job—being a wife.

"Sure you can, dear," she says flippantly. "Besides, Anderson will be there. He's home for the summer. This will be his last year at Yale, you know."

The excitement in her voice is like nails on a chalkboard today. "Mom, Anderson is younger than me. And still in college. You can't be serious."

"Well," she says, sounding offended. For whom, I'm not sure. "I take it you're not coming then?"

I sigh and rub at the ache forming at the base of my neck. "No, Mom. I'm going to have to miss out on this one."

"I hope you don't regret this one day," she says, resigned. "I just want you to find a nice young man and settle down. You're not getting any younger, you know."

"Love you too, Mom." I hang up before she can say anything else. A bubble bath is calling my name.

Thursday's tutoring sessions went even better than Tuesday's. Elli especially did well. She's showing so much more confidence in her answers.

"Great job today," I say, giving her a high five. "You're really good at this math game. I think you will have these facts memorized in no time!"

She blushes and dips her head. "Thanks. I've been practicing."

"You have?" I ask, surprised. When I told Daniel she didn't need to do extra work, it was so she could experience a sense of accomplishment without feeling overwhelmed.

"Yeah, my daddy and I have been playing a game with cards. We have to show two cards and add them up. Whoever has the highest total wins the cards. He said it's kind of like war, but more fun." She grins and reaches into her tote bag. "I tried to teach Liam today, but he didn't like it."

"Oh, that does sound like a fun game to play with your dad." I smile. Daniel really is a great father. Always thinking of Elli's needs. I hope whoever I marry will be as involved in our children's lives as he is in hers.

"Knock, knock."

"Speaking of your dad," I say, shooting him a smile. "Elli was just telling me about your game. I love it!"

Redness creeps up Daniel's neck and splotches on his cheeks. "Thanks. I did an internet search for fun ways to practice math. That was one of them. I had a deck of cards, so we gave it a shot." He shrugs like it's nothing, but I haven't met many dads who would go to those lengths for their kids. Most dads defer to Mom when it comes to schooling. Even my dad left Mom to her own devices. I used to wish he would step in more, but . . .

"That is great." I glance down at Elli who is dropping her cards into her bag. "I'd love to play next time we meet."

"Why don't you come over to our house tonight and play with us?" Elli squeals. "Daddy said it's going to be a pizza night. Do you like pizza?"

Daniel's mouth drops open. "Elli, Ms. Reese probably has better things to do tonight than to come over for pizza and cards."

I'm about to gracefully decline when Elli chimes in.

"Nuh uh, I heard Ms. Reese tell Ms. Morgan that she wasn't going on another date. That she was just going to stay home from now on."

Is it hot in here? My face feels like it's on fire. I wave a hand furiously in front of my face as if by some miracle that will stop me from looking like a ripe tomato. "I . . ." I stammer. Words have escaped me. "Uhm." I try to swallow, but my mouth is suddenly as dry as the Sahara.

"Elli!" Daniel finally booms. "You shouldn't repeat that kind of stuff. It was private, I'm sure."

Elli looks from me to her dad, her eyes shimmering with unshed tears. "I'm sorry," she says as she starts to cry in earnest. "I didn't know it was private."

I can't help it. I drop to my knees and pull her into my arms. "It's okay, Elli. I should remember that little ears can hear everything, even when you don't think they are listening."

Elli sniffles and wipes her nose with the back of her hand. I dig through the cart sitting beside me and rip off a paper towel I keep for "just in case" moments like these, and hand it to her.

"You're not mad at me?" She hiccups the words out, breaking my heart.

"No, I'm not." I smile at her and take the paper towel back to wipe her tears. "I was a little embarrassed, but I'm not mad."

A wobbly smile pulls at Elli's lips. "So, you'll come have pizza and play cards with us?"

"I'm not sure your daddy meant that he wanted to have company tonight. Some things are just for family." I pat her back and push her hair from her wet face.

"It's fine with me," Daniel says, looking from me to Elli and back again. "If you don't have plans already, that is."

"Please, Ms. Reese," Elli begs. "I really want you to."

"Sure." I'm agreeing before my brain catches up. My heart dances in my chest. *Traitor.* "I'll need to run home first, but text me your address. I'll be over soon."

"Yay!" Elli dances in place. "Daddy, send her our address." She grabs her bag and takes his hand.

"We usually order pepperoni is that good for you?" Daniel asks.

"Yep, my favorite." I wink at Elli. It's not her fault all my dates have been bad. Who knew dating would be so difficult? You'd think with technology at our fingertips, we'd match with Mr. Perfect in no time. Unfortunately, all I've found is Mr. Perfectly Wrong for me.

"All right, see you in a bit." Daniel takes Elli's bag and turns to go. "We are going to have a little chat about not putting people on the spot."

I stand rooted in place watching them leave. What am I doing? Going to play cards with the sweetest little girl and her dad. This isn't a date. It's just ... I have no idea what it is.

CHAPTER NINE

Daniel

I TAKE A DEEP breath as we step into the evening air. "Elli," I sigh.

"I know, Daddy." She looks at her feet. "I shouldn't have told you about Ms. Reese and her bad dates."

"No, you shouldn't have." I open the door to the truck and help her inside. "You have detective ears, and you hear too much. Even so, that doesn't mean we always share it, okay?"

"I know. Mommy says I ears-drop too much." She shakes her head.

I throw my head back and laugh. "Ears-drop," I repeat.

Elli looks at me like I've lost my mind. Maybe I have, inviting Reese over tonight after that display.

"Elli girl, I think you mean 'eavesdrop.'" I chuckle as I toss her bag onto the floorboard and close her door.

Climbing into the driver's seat, I settle in and start the truck before taking a glance at Elli. "You'll have to help me get everything ready since you invited a friend over."

She nods. "I will."

When we pull into the driveway, Elli's out of the truck as soon as I park. "You're in a hurry," I say, grabbing her bag that she's left behind and getting out. "Where's the fire?"

Elli laughs. "There's no fire, Daddy, but we need to hurry. Ms. Reese is coming and we aren't ready."

Twenty-five minutes later, the pizza is ordered, the cards are in a pile on the table, and Elli is excitedly watching the front window. "She's here!" Elli jumps down from her perch on the chair and races to the front door. "Can I open it, Daddy, please?"

I nod, and she swings the door open just as Reese is stepping onto the small porch outside the front door. "Ms. Reese! You came," Elli throws her arms around Reese's middle.

"I told you I would," Reese says, sending me a puzzled look. "I hope you don't mind," she says, holding out a box of cookies. "I had some left from our baking session on Monday and thought they'd be a perfect desert."

"Elli," I say gently, pulling her out of the doorway. "Why don't we let Reese in the house?"

Elli steps back and smiles. "Want to see my room?" She takes Reese's hand and starts off to her bedroom.

The doorbell rings, grabbing my attention. "I'll get that." I mutter as Elli practically drags Reese down the hallway.

I handle getting the pizza from the delivery person and take it into the dining room. I set a stack of plates and napkins out earlier, so it's ready to eat.

I head down the hallway to rescue Reese only to stop short in Elli's doorway. Reese is sitting cross-legged on the floor, and Elli is draping a cape around Reese's shoulders. She has a sparkly, gem-covered crown on her head, and the scene takes my breath away. A pang of want beats in my heart.

"Hey, ladies," I say when Reese catches me standing in the doorway. "Pizza's here." I try to smile, but I rub the aching spot in my chest instead. This was such a bad idea. Having her in my house is seriously blurring the lines I'm trying to draw. Her scent lingers in every room she's walked through. I'm in trouble.

"Pizza!" Elli says excitedly. "It's my favorite thing ever."

"I thought you said *I* was your favorite thing ever," I tease, grateful to get the spotlight back where it belongs, and away from the feelings I am not ready to think about.

Elli grabs my hand and pulls me from her room. "Ugh, Dad," she drawls. "You know you're my favorite Daddy, but pizza is my favoritest food ever."

"Good to know," I chuckle. "Ready to eat?" I ask Reese. To my surprise, she stands and comes our way, leaving the crown and cape on.

"Of course." She dips into a curtsy. "A princess must keep up her energy."

Elli giggles. I can feel my eyes crinkle when my lips curve up into a smile. When's the last time I smiled this much?

Several pieces of pizza and Elli-giggles later we are preparing to play the version of war I found online. "Two games, then it's bedtime." I try to keep Elli on a schedule. Especially since we have to make it to Brant and Morgan's before I head into work.

"Aw, Dad," Elli whines. "That's not enough."

Reese takes her crown off and sets it on the table beside her. "That has to be plenty," she says calmly. "I have to go home then so I can be in bed on time."

"*You* have a bedtime?" Elli asks, surprised. "I thought grown-ups could do whatever they wanted."

Reese nods her head. "I do have a bedtime. I have to get up early for school every day too, you know. Even in the summer, I try to keep

the same bed time. It makes it easier when school starts back."
She winks at me.

"Okay!" Elli grabs the cards and deals them out. "Let's get
started then. Ms. Reese and I will play first, and then Daddy, you
can play the winner."

"Sounds good. I'm going to go grab the cookies so we can
have dessert while we play." I can hear Elli telling Reese the
rules as I make my way into the kitchen to grab the container
Reese brought with her. I pause for a moment. This is what I
dreamed of when Heather and I got married. Sitting around the
table laughing, playing games with our children. Not splitting
time and co-parenting.

I sigh. Nothing to be done about it now.

"Here we go," I say, setting the open container in the middle
of the table. "I brought some napkins too."

"Thanks, Daddy." Elli grins and holds her cards close to her
chest. "My turn first, right? You said it goes from youngest to
oldest."

I laugh. "Yep, them's the rules."

Elli lays down her two cards and takes a minute to add them
up. "Five and ten, that's fifteen."

Reese flips over her first two cards. "Twelve."

"I win!" Elli grabs Reese's cards and adds them to her used
card pile.

I munch on cookies and watch as the game progresses. Elli
struggles a bit a time or two, but figures out the addition pretty
quickly.

"This is it," Reese says, flipping over her last two cards. "Ten.
I win that round. Time to count our cards."

"I have eighteen," Elli says, frowning. "That means you win.
Daddy said whoever has more than twenty-six wins."

"That was a really fun game. I can tell you're getting faster with your math facts already," Reese praises as she gathers all the cards into a pile.

"Thank you," Elli says, remembering her manners. "Now you play, Daddy."

"We don't have to play. I'm sure you'd like to have some alone time with your dad before bed."

Elli shakes her head. "Them's the rules," she says echoing her father. "Daddy plays the winner."

"Oh, okay." Reese looks at me questioningly. "If you're sure ..."

"Yep, them's the rules," I repeat. I take the cards and start to shuffle. "Elli, why don't you go brush your teeth and get your pajamas on while we set up the game?"

"Aww, Dad, do I have to?" Elli is the queen of stalling at bedtime. One more drink, one more story, one more ... anything.

"Yes," I say, pointing to the hallway. "It's getting late already."

"Okay," Elli stands and drags her feet all the way to the bathroom.

"Thanks for coming over tonight." I set the cards in front of me since we have a few minutes before Elli is back. "Elli hasn't stopped talking about you since I picked her up on Monday. It seems you've made a new friend."

Reese smiles, a hint of pink highlights her freckles. It's adorable, and I find myself wanting to know how many she has.

"Elli's a great kid. She just needs a confidence boost and a little extra practice. This game is wonderful, by the way. I may need to use it in my tutoring sessions."

"Feel free. I wouldn't have thought to look for math games, except Elli was talking about the game you showed her and said she'd had fun playing it."

Elli races back into the room, her Elsa nightgown leaving little bits of glitter on the floor behind her. I sigh. Looks like I'll be sweeping up the floor and changing her sheets again. I need to remember, no glitter on nightgowns.

"You didn't start without me, did you?" she asks, panting. "I hurried as fast as I could."

"Nope, we waited just for you."

Elli grins. "Ms. Reese, I think you go first, right?"

"Um, I guess so?" Reese blushes again. "I don't know how old your dad is, but I'm twenty-four."

"Oh, then you definitely go first. My daddy is way older than that." Elli's eyes open wide, as if to emphasize her point.

"Hey!" I say laughing. "I'm not that old."

"You're thirty-four," Elli says, nodding her head. "That's old. You're even older than Grandma."

"What? I'm not older than Grandma, Elli. That's impossible." Where does she come up with this stuff?

"You are too! Grandma said she hasn't gotten a day older since she turned thirty." Elli puts her little hands on her hips. "So you're older than Grandma."

Laughter floats from behind the hand Reese is using to cover her mouth.

"Elli, Grandma is fifty-six. She may not accept it, but that's the truth."

Elli frowns. "Hmm."

"All right," I say, still chuckling. "Let's start. Reese, you are younger by a couple of years, so you can go first."

Her eyebrows raise. "Just a couple." She grins and lays down her first two cards.

Elli never lets the conversation lag, and I find I'm having more fun playing cards with Reese and Elli than I've had in a long time. Maybe my mom is right. Maybe I should open myself up to the possibility of another relationship. It's been nice having someone here to talk to and share a meal with.

My eyes catch Reese's green ones and my breath hitches. No. She's too young; I'm sure we'd have nothing in common. I'm certainly not going down that road again. Heather and I thought our love would overcome having nothing in common. Turns out, that difference only gets more pronounced after you have a child. We had nothing but Elli to hold us together, and in the end, it wasn't enough.

"You win!" Elli jumps up and rushes to Reese's side of the table. "You win! You beat Daddy." She throws her arms around Reese and squeezes.

Reese hugs her back. "Thanks for inviting me over to play with you tonight. I had fun."

Elli nods her head. "I knew you would. Pizza night is my favorite."

I finish putting the deck of cards back into the box, and stand up. "All right, Elli girl, time to head to bed."

"But I want to walk Ms. Reese to the door. Grandma says to be a good hostess you walk your guest to the door."

"Grandma's been sharing a lot of wisdom with you lately, I see. Okay, you can walk Ms. Reese to the door, but then it's bedtime. No excuses."

Elli claps her hands excitedly. "Okay, Daddy."

Reese gets her purse from the counter where she'd stashed it, and we walk her to the door. It's awkward now. Do we hug? Shake hands? I'm not sure what to do here.

"Thanks for inviting me," Reese says again. "I'll see you guys this weekend at Brant and Morgan's?"

"Yeah," I say, stuffing my hands into my pockets. "We'll be there."

"Bye, Ms. Reese. See you this weekend." Elli waves as Reese turns to step out the door.

"Wait," I say. "Did you want to take some pizza home? There were some leftovers." I realize I'm not ready for her to go.

"It's okay," she says, winking at Elli. "I happen to know they won't go to waste."

"That's true." I sigh and consider just asking her to stay longer. She'd already told Elli she has a bed time, and I've got no idea how I'd explain her staying to Elli.

"Thanks again for having me over." Reese steps outside and turns to wave.

"My pleasure," I say, and I mean it. Having her here felt natural. Like she belongs here.

"Bye, Ms. Reese," Elli calls out again before rushing to the living room and peeking out the front window.

"Drive safe," I call just as she reaches her car.

"Will do." She waves one last time and I close the door.

"Time for bed Elli."

Elli drags her feet toward the hallway. "Will you still read me a story?"

"Of course. Grab a book and get comfortable. I'll be right in." I grab the cookie container, snap the lid back into place, and take it into the kitchen.

"And you'll do all the voices?"

"We'll see," I say, sighing. "Is there a book about little girls who won't go to bed?"

She giggles. "I don't think so, Daddy—that would be boring."

I chuckle to myself. Of course it would.

Chapter Ten

Reese

I BRUSH FLOUR FROM my nose and check the recipe card again. Hmm, I wonder how important it is to use that brand of cornmeal. Shrugging, I add the egg and mix. Why did I choose to bring my grandmother's cornbread to a cookout? I should have made my pasta salad. Too late now I think, looking at the clock.

I pour the batter into the hot, greased cast iron skillet and slide it into the oven. Fingers crossed I didn't mess this up. I set the timer on the oven, and hope for the best.

An hour later, the cornbread is cool and waiting by the stove, and I'm showered and ready to go. I place a hand over my racing heart. It's just a get-together with friends. No need to be so anxious. Ha!

I look down at my jean shorts and lace-trimmed t-shirt, wondering if I should change for the third time. My fingers find the edge of the shirt and rub. I sigh. I've given this way too much thought.

I pull down a platter, and flip the corn bread onto the large round plate. A hand-me-down from my mother. A good southern woman has to be prepared in order to be a good hostess. No paper plates and plastic forks for my mom. Although, I've found very few people actually care about that.

I wrap the whole plate in foil, making sure to leave a vent on the edge—don't want the cornbread getting soggy—and grab my purse. I balance the plate on my hip as I close and lock the door to my apartment. Taking a deep breath, I let it out slowly.

I can do this.

By the time I pull into the driveway at Brant and Morgan's, I'm feeling more in control of myself. Thankfully.

What could go wrong? It's just friends having food and hanging out. Not like it's another nightmare date. I shudder. Just once, I'd like to go on a date where the guy's attention is on me, and not himself.

Stepping out of the car, I slide my purse strap over my arm and lean in to grab the cornbread platter from the passenger seat.

"Need help?"

At the sound of Daniel's deep voice, I jump and slam my head into the roof of the car. "Ouch!"

"Oh, shoot. Sorry I scared you. Are you okay?" he asks, his voice soft with concern.

Daniel guides me from the car and runs his hands along the top of my head. "I'm fine," I say, more to get him to stop touching me than because I believe it. The way my heart is kicking around in my chest right now, I'm most definitely not fine. I think that has more to do with Daniel's callused hands on my scalp and face than it does the actual knot I can feel forming.

"If you're sure . . ." he says, looking into my eyes as though he is checking for a concussion.

I laugh and wave him off. "Of course. I've bumped my head much harder than that before." Okay, that might not have been the thing to say. Daniel's face is drawn in with that look of fatherly concern. Heat burns through my neck and up my cheeks.

"I'll take that inside. You take it easy today, okay?" Daniel reaches for the platter and turns toward the house.

"Yes, sir," I say jokingly.

Daniel turns and pins me with a look that has me squirming in place. "I mean it. Head injuries can be sneaky."

"I'm sorry," I manage. "I'll take it easy."

He nods and waits for me to close the car door and catch up before walking inside with me.

Instantly, I'm met with the smell of savory bacon cooking and my mouth waters. Morgan is standing at the stove flipping sizzling strips of bacon while Brant is making up burger patties at the counter next to her. Evan leans against the island with a beer in his hand, taking it all in. "Where are the kids?" I ask, looking around.

"They're outside," Morgan says, pointing her spatula towards the double doors. "I didn't want them underfoot when I was cooking. No grease burns today, thank you very much."

Daniel sets my dish on the island with the rest of the food, and grins. "Want to help me fill water balloons for them? Elli has been asking when you were going to get here."

"Um, water balloons?"

Daniel's grin grows wider. "Yep! A special request."

"From whom?" I ask, laughing.

"Me, of course." He winks and makes his way out the sliding glass doors and into the back yard.

"May as well go help him," Evan says, tipping his bottle back and taking a sip. "I heard Elli plans to get us all at some point. Maybe you can intercept her and avoid getting hit." He winks and pushes himself off the counter. "I'm going to go make myself available to Liam's team."

"Good plan." I head outside and am met with giggles. Elli is currently flying high over Daniel's head and laughing hysterically. Liam is dancing from foot to foot nearby. Probably waiting for his turn.

"Whoa there," Evan says before swooping Liam up. "Let's not leave Liam out!" He swings Liam around in the air, his laughter bubbling up like water from a spring. Uninhibited.

I can't help the smile that lights my face. Their joy is infectious. This is so much better than the uptight parties my parents threw when I was growing up.

Deciding to get in on the fun, I sneak off to the side of the house and turn on the water spigot. Grabbing the hose, I set the nozzle to mist before jumping out and spraying them all with water.

Daniel and Evan drop the kids to their feet and throw their hands in front of their faces. Liam and Elli start dancing in the spray. I'm laughing harder than I have in a long, long time when Morgan and Brant step onto the porch.

"What's going on out here?" Brant asks, taking in the sight. "We can hear you laughing clear from the kitchen."

Morgan grins and leans into Brant's side. "Looks like Reese was just helping everyone cool off," she says, laughing.

I put down the hose and go back to the side of the house to turn the water off. As my hand reaches the knob, cool water hits me from behind. I spin in place, my hand in front of my face. "What the . . ."

Daniel is doubled over laughing. "Payback!" he cackles. "Couldn't let you be the only one who stays dry."

"Hey!" I say, laughing and shaking water off my arms. "Brant and Morgan are still dry!"

"Yeah," he says, still chuckling. "But they're making the food."

We make our way to the back porch where Morgan has set out a few towels to dry off with.

"What about the water balloons?" Elli asks excitedly.

"I think we got wet enough for now," Evan says, wiping water from his face and arms. "Why don't we save those for the lake trip?"

"Okay," Elli says, pouting a bit.

Liam has another idea, and off they go, running through the yard.

"I've been meaning to ask you if you'd like to go with us," Morgan says, dropping into a chair next to me. "We've decided to take a week and rent a cabin at the lake. Evan, Daniel, Elli, Brant, Liam and I are all going to go. We'd love it if you'd join us."

"Oh, when is it?" I ask. "I'll have to see if it works with my tutoring schedule."

"The last week of June. We want to host a Fourth of July party here this year, and we figured the last week of June would be a great time to get away. It'll give us a chance to really relax before July comes and summer winds down."

I nod. Being a teacher means summer comes to an end sooner for me than for the kids. We have meetings and planning sessions, classroom set-up and who knows what else that will be thrown at us starting at the end of July.

"Let me check my schedule and I'll let you know." I'd love to relax by the lake for a week. I'll have to clear it with the parents of my students, but I should be able to take that time off.

The smell of burgers and chicken on the grill makes my stomach grumble.

"Someone's hungry," Daniel says, taking the seat opposite me and putting his feet on the little ottoman in front of him.

I blush. "I didn't eat lunch," I say, tucking a strand of hair behind my ear. "Sorry."

He grins. "For what? Being hungry? I'm starving!" He looks over his shoulder to where Brant is manning the grill. "Almost done over there? Some of us are withering away."

"It's coming; don't rush the cook." Brant waves his tongs at us. "Go inside and have some fruit salad if you can't wait. The meat will be done in a few minutes."

"I'll wait," I say quickly. I learned a long time ago not to make a fuss.

Ten minutes later, we are all lined up around the island making our plates. The smells of the food remind my stomach we skipped lunch and are causing it to protest loudly.

"You should have grabbed a snack," Daniel says softly in my ear, causing shivers to race up my spine and down my arms.

"I'm fine." I take a scoop of baked beans and add it to my plate. "Besides, I need a missed meal now and then."

He scoffs before scooping beans onto his waiting plate. "I don't think so, Reese." His voice is soft and deep, only loud enough for me to hear.

I shrug, not knowing what to say, and not trusting myself to say anything at all. The attraction I've been feeling for Daniel these last few weeks has made it harder and harder to see him as off-limits. But he is. Off-limits. He is Elli's dad, Brant's friend, and ten years older than I am.

I decide I need some space between us and head to the other side of the island to finish filling my plate. Morgan has cut the cornbread into little wedges, and I grab one, placing it on the side of my beans. I just hope it's as good as when my grandma used to make it.

We all head outside and sit on the patio chairs we'd abandoned to make our plates. The kids spread out at a small picnic table in the grass. Conversation flows, and I focus on eating gracefully, slowly, so as not to make a mess and embarrass anyone.

"I'm too hungry for small bites," Morgan says, eyeing me. "I thought you'd dig in, as hungry as you seemed."

I shrug. "Don't want to make a mess."

She laughs. "Girl, we're outside, and this food is supposed to be messy." She winks and takes a bite of her burger, mayonnaise dripping from the bottom of the bun as if to say, *See, it's okay.*

Evan picks up his cornbread, and I pause, waiting for his reaction. He takes a bite and stops chewing. Reaching for his water, he takes a huge gulp and swallows.

Grabbing my cornbread, I pinch a piece off and pop it in my mouth . . . and all I taste is salt. "Ugh!" I grab a napkin and spit the offending bread inside. "Do NOT eat the cornbread!" Tears prick my eyes. I throw the napkin onto my plate and rush inside.

I toss the paper plate into the trash and beeline for the bathroom before the tears start to fall. Locking the door, I turn and slide down its hard surface until my face is in my knees. Wetness rolls down my cheeks and onto my legs. I don't even bother wiping them away.

A soft knock at the door makes me jump. "I'll be out in a minute." I grab for some toilet paper and wipe my eyes. I'm sure my makeup is ruined. Just one more thing to add to the "Reese is an Embarrassment" list.

"Hey," Morgan calls through the closed door, concern dripping from her voice. "It's just cornbread—it's not the end of the world."

"Yeah," I say, throwing the wet tissue into the trash.

"Okay," she says softly, hesitating when I don't say more. "I'll be outside. Join us when you're ready. It's really not a big deal."

"I'll be out soon." I look around the bathroom. No window. Of course not. Life would be so much simpler if I could climb out the window and just disappear.

I should have known better than to bring a dish I made. Mom's always telling me I need to take lessons. I've never been great in the kitchen, but it's cornbread. I followed the recipe. I've made this before and it's been fine. Not this time.

I know I'm overreacting, but it's hard to shake the feeling that I can't do anything right.

CHAPTER ELEVEN

Daniel

MORGAN COMES BACK OUT to the porch after checking on Reese, her face drawn. "She's really upset," she says softly.

"Why?" Evan asks. "It's not even the worst cornbread I've ever had. A bit salty, but meh."

We all eat quietly, waiting for Reese to come back to the group. Five minutes later, she still hasn't rejoined us.

Grabbing my now empty plate, I head inside. It's quiet. Which means Reese is probably still hiding in the bathroom. I head down the hallway and stop just outside the door. The sound of sniffles coming from inside breaks my heart. It's just cornbread to us, but obviously it means much more to her.

"Reese," I call, knocking softly on the door. "Hey, it's me. Open the door, please?" I wait a beat. The sound of feet shuffling is the only noise I can hear. "Okay, don't open the door. Just listen." I pause, hoping she'll at least crack the thing.

Nope. I decide to share an embarrassing story of my own. "The first day I worked with Brant, I got flustered by a customer, and didn't tighten the lug nuts on the tire all the way. Brant noticed the tire wobble as I was backing it out and thankfully was able to stop a disaster from happening."

Still silence.

"I felt awful. I was so embarrassed, and certain that Brant was going to fire me on my first day. It was such a rookie mistake, and I'd been working on cars for years at that point." Seeing she isn't going to open the door, I slide into a sitting position outside the door and keep talking.

"Brant just clapped me on the shoulder and told me to pay attention next time. That was it. I'd like to say I didn't feel like a complete idiot for the next few days, but that wouldn't be the truth. The truth is, mistakes happen. Everyone gets embarrassed. It's how we move forward that matters. And people who really care about you won't care one bit. They may tease you, because humor is a great tension diffuser, but honestly, Reese, none of us care about a little bit of salty cornbread."

The sound of the lock turning has me picking my head up. The door cracks open, and Reese peeks out.

"I'm a mess." Her voice wobbles.

"You're a cute mess." I pause, wishing I could bring those words back. "I mean . . ."

She laughs. "Thanks, Daniel. Really."

I nod, afraid to open my mouth and let anything else come flying out.

"I'll be out in a second. I just want to wipe my face."

She leaves the door open this time, which I take as a good sign. I nod and head back outside.

"Daddy!" Elli yells, running and jumping into my arms. "It's almost time!"

"Time for what?" I ask, teasing her. Now that the sun is starting to set, it's the perfect time to catch fireflies.

"To chase the lightning bugs, silly." She smiles and wiggles down. "Ms. Morgan made us jars with holes in the lids and everything. She said we can only keep them in the jar for a little while, though. Then we have to let them go." She frowns for a second, but like a ghost, the disappointment is gone and excitement takes its place. "Can we chase them now?"

Liam is holding both jars in his hands, just waiting for permission to take off. "Sure," I say, ruffling her hair. "Just be careful and stay out of the woods."

Brant's back yard is huge and edges up to a small patch of woods in the back. I'd hate to have to find them in the dark woods. Today's been eventful enough.

Liam and Elli run off, giggling the whole way as they run towards the back of the yard where they are more likely to spot the fireflies they're looking for. Brant and Evan are busy building a bonfire in the fire pit, and Morgan's moving the deck chairs down to the softly glowing embers.

"Can I help?" I ask, taking a chair.

"That's the last one," she says, smiling. "Would you mind bringing the cooler with the drinks down? That way we can just relax and watch the kids."

"Sure thing."

A few minutes later, Reese has rejoined us, and I'm leaned back with a cold Coke in my hand, sitting by the fire pit watching the kids slowly fill their jars with the blinking bugs. This is my idea of a perfect summer evening.

"Where's your neighbor?" Brant asks Evan.

"I didn't invite her," Evan shrugs. "I told you, she's just the girl next door."

Brant and I laugh.

"I'm not bringing a girl around here unless she's staying mate-rial," Evan says, taking a drink from his bottle of water. "And we all know that isn't happening anytime soon."

I grin. "Famous last words," I say, tipping my can back and taking a drink. It's probably a bit too warm for a fire tonight, but the kids wanted s'mores. Besides, there's something soothing about the smell of burning wood and the crackling logs in the summertime.

Morgan slides a box with marshmallows, chocolate, and gra-ham crackers to Brant. "You're on s'mores duty when the kids are ready."

"Sounds good to me." Brant grins. He really has taken to the role of father figure quickly. I don't think he could love Liam more. Even if he were his biological father.

Conversation dies down, and Reese clears her throat. "I'd like to apologize." She looks at her hands, which are twisting the lace of her shirt. "I made an embarrassment of myself tonight. I'm sorry."

Brant, Evan, Morgan and I exchange looks.

"Nah," Evan says quickly. "You didn't do anything. Besides, you should see the stuff these two do at the shop. Hot messes—both of them." He winks and takes a deep pull from his water bottle. "I'm going to go see who's winning."

"It's not a competition," I holler, but he's already headed for the kids. I shake my head. "He's the hot mess."

Brant laughs and reaches for Morgan's hand. "It's nothing," he says to Reese. "Really."

Reese nods and lets go of her shirt. "Maybe I'll see how many bugs Elli has in her jar."

I watch as she walks away, determined to make the best of the rest of her night. She's stronger than she thinks she is. Somehow, she's gotten under my skin, and I need to figure out how to stop it. Because the more I learn about Reese, the more I want to learn.

The kids tire of chasing the lightning bugs and decide it's time to roast marshmallows for s'mores. Brant slides the marshmallows on the end of the skewers and shows the kids where to stand so they don't get burned.

"I remember this being the highlight of the summer," Evan says, pointing at the two kids now focused on roasting the perfect marshmallow. "Roasting marshmallows, chasing lightning bugs. There was something about being outside and getting dirty in the summertime that was magical."

We all nod, watching the kids as they layer graham crackers, chocolate and marshmallows into a gooey mess.

Thirty minutes later, the kids are covered in sticky, chocolaty goo, and rubbing their eyes.

"All right," I say standing and stretching my back. "I think it's time to get you home, Elli girl."

"But, Dad," Elli whines. A sure sign she's over tired and had enough.

"There will be more time to stay up too late and roast marshmallows at the lake." We say our goodbyes, and head around the front of the house to the truck. I'm helping Elli in when I hear footsteps behind me. I know it's her before she even calls my name. I can feel her.

"Daniel?" Reese waits for me to finish with Elli and close her door.

"Hey." I lean against the truck, waiting for her to gather the courage to say what she needs to. Her hands are back to rubbing the lace on her shirt. She seems to do that when she's nervous. That makes me smile a bit. She's just as off-kilter as I am.

"I wanted to thank you. For earlier."

"It's really nothing," I say, softly. "You'd have done the same."

We stand there for a few moments, neither of us knowing what to say. "Well, I guess I'd better get Elli home and cleaned up."

"Yeah," she tries to smile, but it looks more like a grimace. "I'll see you Tuesday, I guess."

"See you then."

She spins on her heel, and rushes back around the side of the house. I watch her leave. I wish I could figure her out.

After the awkward way Reese and I parted on Saturday, I'm unsure what to expect when I pick Elli up on Tuesday evening. The tutoring sessions seem to be working though, because Elli has been much more eager to read aloud. She appears to be remembering her math facts much faster, too.

I pause outside the door when I hear Elli and Reese laughing together. The sound does something funny to my heart.

I knock softly, and the door swings open revealing a smiling Elli. Her face is flushed with joy. "What are we celebrating?" I ask, raising a brow.

"I just remembered all my subtractions, Daddy!"

I pick her up and swing her around. "This calls for a celebration!" I pull her in for a hug, relieved that the tutoring is helping her. I'd hate for her to start third grade still struggling.

"Can we get burgers and a milkshake?" Elli asks, dancing in place.

"Of course, Elli girl. It's your celebration." I smile as she claps her hands together. "Reese, would you like to join us?" As soon as the invitation is out, my eyes snap to hers. What am I doing?

"Please, Ms. Reese. You have to come!" Elli sticks out her bottom lip and does her best puppy dog eyes. Those eyes have been the cause of way too many ice cream stops over the years.

"Well," Reese hesitates. "Okay."

"Yay! Best day EVER!" Elli hurriedly picks up the remnants of the game they were playing and puts the game back in Reese's wagon.

"Can I help you take these things to your car?" My mom would be disappointed if I didn't offer to help. It's the gentlemanly thing to do. I'd do it for anyone. Not just because I feel drawn to her, I assure myself.

"Sure," Reese gives me a half smile and reaches into her pocket. "Here are my keys. You can just put it in the trunk, if you don't mind."

Our fingers touch as I take the keys from her hand. Her eyes widen and find mine. I linger a bit too long, enjoying the feeling. It's been so long since I reacted to someone, I just want to soak it in for a minute. Even if I have sworn off relationships, and Reese is ten years my junior.

She takes her hand back, wiping it on her denim shorts, and gives a nervous laugh. "I'll be out in just a minute. I need to tell Samantha I'm done for the day."

"C'mon Elli, let's get Ms. Reese's things stored away."

Thirty minutes later, we're seated across from each other at Beats and Eats. Elli and I on one side of the booth, and Reese on the other. A band is setting up on the small stage in the back corner of the diner. Thursday, Friday, and Saturday nights, they host local-ish live bands. Usually it's just some high school kids who have big dreams of landing a contract, but most of the time they are decent to listen to.

"My mommy said she might come back soon," Elli shares. "I think she misses me." Her little hand is tapping away at the table as the drummer warms up.

Reese grins at her from across the table. "Of course she does—you're a pretty fantastic kid."

Elli preens under the praise. "Daddy, do you miss me when I'm with Mommy?" Elli asks, watching me with laser focus.

"Of course," I say, trying to keep my emotions in check. Elli hasn't ever asked that before. Maybe Heather's trip has made her more aware of our situation. "But I know you're in good hands with your mom. She loves you to the moon."

"I know," she shrugs. "Sometimes, I wish we were all in the same place."

Before I can say anything in response, the waiter is at the table with our food and Elli's milkshake. "Perfect timing," I say, letting out a big sigh.

I glance across the table to Reese, who's stayed silent through the whole interaction. I don't blame her—I wouldn't know what to say either. She gives me a tentative smile.

"My milkshake!" Elli squeals, sliding the straw into the thick, sweet drink and taking a big gulp.

Reese laughs and just like that, the tension is gone.

Thankfully, we get our food and are ready to pay by the time the band is really into their set. Unfortunately, Slim and the Sidewinders isn't the best act I've seen at Beats and Eats.

"Thanks for coming tonight," I say as we walk Reese to her car.

"I had fun." She smiles. "Even if the band could have used a bit more practice."

Elli giggles. "They weren't very good," Elli says quietly. "But don't tell them, 'kay? Their feelings might get hurt. It's not easy to be bad at something in front of other people."

Reese bends down and hugs Elli close. "You know what? You're right, it's not. But the only way to get better at something is to practice. If we really want something, we have to work for it, and accept help when we need it."

And just like that, my heart cracks open a little bit more.

CHAPTER TWELVE

Reese

LUGGING MY HEAVY SUITCASE to my car, I push it into my back seat. I'm so excited about this lake trip. Though I'll avoid making any cornbread. I shake out my arms and shut the door just as my phone rings in my back pocket. I let out a long sigh before grabbing it and swiping to answer.

"Hi, Mom," I say, trying to keep the annoyance out of my voice. She knows I'm headed to the lake this week. She wasn't thrilled I was choosing to go away with friends rather than spend it with her and Dad.

"Hi, dear," Mom says, her voice ringing in my ear. "I was just thinking you might have changed your mind about coming home."

I sigh. "No, Mom. I'm still going to the lake with Morgan and her family." I hate disappointing her, but I've been really looking forward to this getaway.

"I see," Mom says, sadness clear in her voice. "I just don't understand why you'd want to spend your vacation with someone else's family and not your own."

My fingers rub the space between my eyebrows where pressure is building into a headache. This is not how I wanted to start my day.

"They're my friends, and they invited me along. It sounded like a wonderful way to decompress before the school year starts. I promise I'll come visit soon."

My mom's sigh causes a pang of guilt in my stomach. "All right, dear," she says, her tone indicating her disappointment in me. Again. "At least I know you'll be at the annual Fourth of July celebration."

Oh crap. "Um, yeah." I'm not ready to open that can of worms. How do you tell your mom you'd rather spend the holiday with friends than trying to be the perfect daughter?

After a few more loops on the guilt trip roller coaster, I remind Mom I've got to go. "Brant and Morgan are waiting on me, Mom. I don't want to make them late."

"Well, okay then," Mom says abruptly. "Speak soon."

The dial tone sounds before I'm even able to say goodbye. Sitting in the driver's seat of my old Honda Accord, I lay my head on the steering wheel and let out a long breath. I almost decide to call off the lake house trip. Almost.

I'm twenty-four. I shouldn't feel guilty about wanting to spend time with my friends.

With renewed resolve, I start the car and make the ten-minute drive to the Anderson's home.

Morgan and Brant are busy loading the back of their truck with totes and suitcases when I pull up.

"Hey," Morgan calls as I step out of the car. "Right on time."

I blow out a breath. "Barely," I say, raising an eyebrow. "If my mom had her way, I'd be halfway to her house by now." I try to laugh, but it comes out sounding more like a strangled donkey.

"I get it." Morgan grabs my bag from me and passes it to Brant. "It's part of the reason William and I left Florida. Sometimes there's such a thing as too close."

"Ms. Reese, are you ready to swim with us?" Liam has his life vest on and is bouncing in place with all the energy of a kid who's got big plans.

"Sure am!" I say, smiling and crouching down to his level. "Are you planning to wear that in the truck, too?"

Liam laughs and shakes his head. "Nah, but Mommy wanted to make sure it fitted before we leaved."

"Come here," Morgan says, reaching for the straps on the life vest. "Let's get this packed up and we can get on the road. How's that sound?"

"Yay!" Liam shouts. "Daddy, can you help me get buckled?"

Brant's smile stretches wide across his face. "You bet," he says, swooping Liam up and helping him into the truck.

I risk a glance at Morgan, unsure how she feels about Liam calling Brant "Daddy." She's wiping a tear from the corner of her eye when she notices me looking. "He just started calling him Daddy recently. I didn't realize how much it would affect me."

I nod. "I'm sure it's a lot."

"It is," she says, letting out a long breath. "But I couldn't ask for a better father figure for Liam than Brant. William would be happy to know that Liam has such a great role model in his life."

Brant steps back from the truck and closes Liam's door. "Ready, ladies?" he asks. If he heard our conversation, he doesn't let it show.

"All set," we say in tandem.

Liam chatters excitedly the entire way to the lake house. I'm thankful for the noise. I need a distraction from my mom's guilt trip and the butterflies I feel when I think of my week with Daniel.

"Elli and me are gonna go fishing." Liam pretends to cast a line. "Do you like fishing, Ms. Reese?"

"I do," I say hesitantly. It's not a lie, I do like fishing. I just don't enjoy baiting the line.

"Mommy doesn't like to fish at all, right, Mommy?"

Morgan's laugh filters back from the front seat. "Nope. I'd rather lie on the shore and read a book."

Liam shakes his head as though it's the saddest thing he's heard all day. "Who wants to read when you can fish?"

I'm saved from having to answer when we pull into the long, wooded drive that leads back to the cabin we rented for the week. Liam's eyes are round with awe as we approach the massive structure that looks more like a mini mansion than a cabin.

"Whoa!" he whispers. "It's HUGE!"

He's not wrong. I know Morgan and Brant said there was enough space to sleep eight, but from the looks of it, there may be that many bedrooms.

"There's no way I don't owe you more for this," I say, shooting Morgan a frown.

"Don't be silly," she says, waving a hand in dismissal. "You already gave me plenty. Besides, we got a great deal."

Brant puts the truck in park and cuts the ignition. "Well," he says, stretching in his seat, "who's ready to explore?"

"Me!" Liam shouts, already undoing his chest strap. "Ms. Reese, can you do the bottom button?"

"Of course." I push the release, and the buckle slides open. Liam jumps into Brant's arms the moment the door opens.

Stepping out of the truck, I pause a moment to take it all in. Dark wood panels line the front of the home with natural stone accents. The front porch is huge, extending the length of the front of the house. Rocking chairs and colorful potted plants give the expanse a welcoming feel.

Brant unlocks the deep green door, and Liam runs inside.

"WOW!" Liam yells. "You can see the lake outside!"

Following Morgan inside, I look around. The front door opens to a huge open-concept living space with large comfortable-looking furniture. But the focal point is the view.

Liam wasn't kidding. The back wall of the dining room and kitchen is all windows; behind the house, the expanse of the lake stretches out to the mountains on the far side, giving the illusion that we're the only ones here.

"It's stunning." I run my hand along the granite countertops and sigh. This is going to be a fabulous week.

"Yoo-hoo, anyone in here?" Evan comes around the corner, Elli and Daniel trailing behind him. "This place is epic!"

"You're not wrong," Brant says. "The pictures didn't do this place justice." He pushes open a sliding glass door I didn't notice, and steps out onto a wooden deck.

"C'mon, Liam," Elli says, grabbing his little hand. "Let's go look at the bedrooms!"

As they race down the hall, giggles trailing behind them, I smile. It's nice to see them being kids and having fun.

Vacations used to be so stressful when I was a kid. We'd always go with friends of my parents, and I was expected to be seen and not heard. Most of the time, I was the only child. My parents had me a bit later in life, and all their friends either didn't have kids, or their kids were much older than I was. I spent a lot of time in my imagination.

"You better go claim a room," Daniel says, chuckling. "Those two will try to pick the best one for themselves."

"I'm fine wherever," I say, smiling. "The couch is probably better than the bed I have at home. This place is amazing."

"It is," Daniel agrees. "I can't wait to get outside and explore."

Brant, Evan, and Morgan all step back inside, closing the slider behind them.

"Better get unloaded," Brant says to Evan and Daniel. Leaning in, he plants a soft kiss on Morgan's cheek. "Why don't the two of you check on the kids and make sure we actually have beds to sleep in tonight?"

For one moment, I am jealous. I want that kind of love. The way Brant looks at Morgan, like she is his whole world, makes my heart ache. My eyes involuntarily find Daniel. He's already walking out with Brant but turns and catches my eye. I blush when he winks, and when he turns back around, my stomach drops to my knees.

"C'mon," Morgan says, motioning for me to go first. "Let's go figure out sleeping arrangements."

After inspecting the four bedrooms, it's decided that Brant and Morgan get the main suite. Daniel and Evan will bunk together in an enormous room that boasts two double beds. Liam and Elli will share the smaller room with two twins, and I'll get a room to myself. I offered to share with Liam so that Daniel and Elli could have their own space, but they turned me down.

Once the guys drop off all the bags in the appropriate rooms, they offer to take the kids on a walk to inspect the lake access. Morgan and I decide to unload the coolers and food totes while they are gone.

"I'm so glad you came," Morgan says, while putting things into the pantry. "I'd have been the only woman here."

"I'm sure it wouldn't have been too bad. It seems like the guys are excited to spend time with the kids outdoors." I shrug. "I am glad you invited me, though. This is the perfect place to unwind before summer winds down."

Morgan leans against the countertop. "I agree." She opens her mouth as if she is going to say something, and then snaps it shut.

"What's wrong?" I ask. "I've seen that face before. The 'I want to say something, but probably shouldn't' face. You make it during staff meetings, and sometimes during parent-teacher meetings, too." I laugh. "Out with it."

Morgan's cheeks turn a pale shade of pink. "I wasn't going to say anything yet, but . . ." She looks outside to where the men are showing the kids how to skip rocks, and sighs. "Well, you're my co-teacher and my friend."

My fingers find the hem of my shirt. Morgan's making me nervous, and I'm not sure why. "Um, okay," I say, hoping that it will encourage her to keep talking.

"Brant and I have decided to try for a baby." Morgan's face is flaming red, and her eyes shoot down to her feet. "I think that when—if—a baby comes, I'll want to stop working for a while."

I squeal and rush to her, enveloping her in a hug. "I know that is an enormous step for you," I say, stepping back. "I'll miss working with you every day, but I hope you know I support you no matter what."

Morgan lets out a breath and meets my eyes. A smile breaks out across her face. "It's huge. I'm scared, but excited. Life doesn't offer guarantees, and we have to embrace the time we have. I just never thought I'd have any more kids after . . . well—"

I rub my hand across her back. "I know," I say softly. "Sometimes the plans we make for ourselves aren't the plans life hands us." I pause, soaking in what I just said. It's true. Maybe the plans I had for the "perfect" husband and future aren't the ones I'm supposed to have.

My eyes find Daniel down by the lake. He's kneeling down, showing Elli something in his hand. It looks like he's explaining what makes a good skipping rock. My heart races in my chest. Maybe, just maybe, I should listen to my own advice.

Chapter Thirteen

Daniel

I CAN FEEL SOMEONE staring at me, so I look over my shoulder. The reflection of the sun off the lake makes it impossible to see inside. I shrug. If the ladies want us, they can step out onto the deck and call for us.

I turn my attention back to Elli. "Here, watch me." I flick my wrist and skip the rock across the smooth surface of the lake. "Now you try." I look around for the perfect stone. "This rock is nice and smooth, so when you flick your wrist like this, so it spins as it flies, it should skip across the surface of the water." I hand her the small stone. "Try it."

Elli flicks her wrist, and the stone hops twice before sinking into the blue water below.

"I did it!" she yells. "Can I keep trying?"

"Great job," I tell her, handing her another stone. "You'll have to find your own rocks and don't get too close to the edge or you'll get your shoes wet."

"Okay," she says, running to where Brant has just shown Liam what to do. Brant and Evan join me at the water's edge, and we watch the kids try their hand at rock skipping.

"It's funny," Evan says. "The things I enjoyed about the lake as a kid are some of the same things I enjoy now."

I nod in agreement. "Only, it's more fun when you have your own kid. There's something about seeing the excitement through a child's eyes that brings the fun to a deeper level." I'd always imagined having more kids. Maybe a son who'd like to throw the ball around, go to baseball games with. I shake off the thought before sadness can creep in.

"Speaking of," Brant says, rocking back on his heels. "I, uh, well . . . that is . . . Morgan and I . . ." He rubs his hand on the back of his neck and drops his arms to his sides heavily. "Well, we're thinking about having another kid."

"Whoa!" Evan says, his eyes wide with surprise. "You sure you want to do that? Kids are so much work! Especially when they're babies. They eat, sleep, poop, and cry, right?"

I laugh and give Evan a light shove. "Babies are wonderful, Evan. You just need to grow up a bit more and you'll understand." I laugh when he shakes his head. "Seriously, Brant, that's exciting!"

"Thanks. I don't know if it will happen, but we've been talking about it since Christmas and we've decided to give it a shot. I told her it was her decision, and I meant it, but I can't help but be excited to add to our family."

"That's awesome," I pat his back. "I'm happy for you. Maybe next summer, there will be another little one to bring to the lake."

"Yeah, well, don't ask me to babysit," Evan says, his hands raised in front of himself. "I don't do diapers, man."

"Noted." Brant and I laugh.

"Hey, guys," Morgan calls from the porch. "Why don't you come inside and get changed? I was thinking the kids might like to swim a bit before dinner."

"YEAH!" Liam and Elli yell, dropping the rocks they're holding into a pile and racing toward the house.

"Guess we're going swimming."

The next morning, the kids are still worn out from our swim the afternoon before, so we agree to try something new. The lake house has a shed with canoes, fishing poles, life vests, and tubes. We decide to take out the canoes.

Evan and Reese pair up, leaving me with Elli, and Brant with Morgan and Liam. We all put on life vests and get into the canoes. I show Elli how to help steer and off we go. Evan and Reese take off ahead of the group. Brant and Morgan aren't far behind. Elli and I trail back a bit. One adult and an eight-year-old who's never done this before means it's a little more of an indirect path through the water.

"Look, Daddy," Elli says, pointing to something on a log floating in the water. "A turtle."

"I see," I say, trying to guide us a little closer.

Elli's paddle slaps the water, and the turtle slips off the log and back into the water. "Oops." Her face falls.

"Let's see what else we can find." We glide through the water quietly while Elli's eyes scan the shoreline.

"Do you think we might find treasure?" Elli asks, her face scrunched in concentration.

"Probably not here," I say, laughing. "This part of the lake has seen a lot of visitors, so they have probably already found any treasure."

"Oh." She sighs. "That stinks."

The sound of Reese's rich throaty laughter skips across the water and straight into my heart. My head whips in her direction. Evan has his hands in the air like he is telling her a story, and her head is tossed back, hair floating in gorgeous red waves behind her.

Suddenly, I'm irrationally jealous. Evan shouldn't be making her laugh. It should be me. I shake the thought away as soon as it comes. Elli is my world. I can't risk her heart again. Especially since she has voiced this summer that she wishes her mom and I could live together again like one big happy family. Besides, Evan knows I'm working through some things where Reese is concerned.

There's a pull, something I can't quite stop with Reese. I just don't know if I'm ready to put my heart, and Elli's, on the line again.

After some time on the lake, I turn Elli and myself back toward the shore. It's exhausting paddling this thing around by myself. Plus, I don't think I can watch Evan make Reese laugh anymore. It's driving me crazy.

"Hey, Elli girl, how about we head back and start getting lunch together?" I'm appealing to her sense of hunger. The girl may be eight, but she eats like a teenager.

"Sure," she shrugs. "My arms are getting tired from paddling, anyway."

I do my best to hold in the laugh that wants to break free. "I understand," I say instead.

We are just dragging the canoe onto the bank when Brant and Morgan paddle in.

"Elli and I are going to get lunch started. I figured we'll let the canoes dry a bit before we put them back in the shed." I dust my hands off on my pants.

"Sounds good to me," Brant says, hopping out and helping Morgan and Liam to dry land. "I'll drag this up a bit and be right in to help. I'm starving."

"I'll beat ya!" Liam yells, taking off in a sprint toward the house.

"Nuh uh," Elli shouts, following close behind him.

"They certainly are enjoying themselves," Morgan says, watching them race toward the back of the house. "I think this is exactly what we all needed."

Morgan makes a platter of sandwiches while I cut up a watermelon. Brant and the kids set the table and get drinks for everyone. I can't help peeking out the enormous windows looking for Reese and Evan.

"They'll be back." Morgan hands the food to Brant before pinning me with a knowing look. "A word of advice." She pauses. "Reese is a really sweet woman, and she has dreams of forever and kids. If that's not something you could see yourself with . . ." She shakes her head. "Just don't hurt her. She's been through enough."

I don't know what to say, so I just nod and make my way to the table.

The kids have already made their plates, and are talking about what they want to do next.

"I think it's a great time to relax," Morgan points out. "This afternoon we are going to explore some trails, so you'll need your energy."

The kids are laid out in the living room watching the latest animated movie about talking pets when Evan and Reese come back into the house.

"We put some sandwiches in the fridge for you guys. There's a bowl of watermelon in there too." Morgan points to the kitchen. "I think I'm going to go take a nap. Brant?"

Brant stretches his arms above his head and lets out a yawn. "A nap sounds good to me."

"Me too," I say, standing and stretching one arm, then the other. "I'll just go let the kids know to stay inside and come get us if they need anything."

"Oh," Reese says from the kitchen. "I can stay with them." She picks up her plate piled high with watermelon and sandwich squares. "I'm actually not tired." She shrugs. "Plus, I've seen this movie. It's actually really cute."

"You've seen a kids' movie?" Evan asks, his eyebrows coming together in confusion.

Reese laughs. "I'm a preschool teacher," she says and pops a cube of watermelon into her mouth on her way to the living room.

"Weird," Evan says, grabbing his food. "I'm going out to eat on the deck. I need to call Karlee and see if she's checked on Mittens."

Huh, I've never known Evan to call and check up on Mittens before. Maybe there is something with the girl next door after all.

I stand in the kitchen a moment longer debating whether I should push through and watch the rest of the movie with Reese and the kids, or take the nap I so desperately want. Turns out, Evan snores. Loudly. Between thinking of Reese being in the room right next door, and his inability to sleep quietly, I didn't get much sleep last night. Morgan's words echo through my head, and I decide a nap sounds fantastic right about now.

Two hours later, we are all refreshed and ready to explore Hawkins Trail. We all agreed taking the easiest trail with the kids was the smartest idea. Plus, the other two trails are named Rattlesnake

Pass and Black Bear Trail—a little more intimidating for the under ten crowd.

Brant, Evan, and I have backpacks filled with water, bug spray, first aid supplies, and a map of the trails, just in case.

"Stick close, and watch for snakes." Elli and Liam are already out in front, leading the way. I'm sure they are making enough noise to scare off any wildlife, but you never know.

"Maybe you guys should let a grown-up lead," Morgan says timidly.

"They'll be all right," Brant says, bringing their entwined fingers to his lips and kissing her knuckles.

She visibly relaxes and leans into him. "If you're sure."

I glance at Reese who is watching the interaction with longing written all over her face. Morgan's right; she wants it all. She deserves it too.

I hang back a bit until I'm at the back of the pack, lost in my own thoughts. What would I have to offer someone if I did open up and let a woman in? I don't want to go all in and have it torn away again. It wouldn't be fair. Not to Elli, and not to me, either.

Reese is young, and I learned my lesson about being in a relationship with someone when you have little in common. Bad idea.

Although, she hasn't complained once so far on this trip. She didn't even flinch when I told the kids to watch for snakes. Her age doesn't even come to mind when we are all sitting around talking and joking.

Even if I decided to take a chance, she deserves someone her own age. So why does that idea make my gut churn?

The sound of Elli shouting snaps me out of my thoughts. I run to catch up. "What's wrong? What happened?" Brant is helping a crying Elli to her feet. "What happened?" I repeat.

"She fell," Morgan says softly. "She tripped over that root, and fell hard onto her hands and knees."

I make my way past the group to where Elli is standing, Brant examining her hands and knees. "Good thing we wore pants," he says. "Not a scrape on the knees at all, but your hands have a few minor scratches."

"I want to go back," Elli cries. "I don't like hiking."

I set down my pack, and pull out some water and the first aid kit. "Let me rinse your hands."

Elli shakes her head and yanks her hands back to her sides. "No! It will hurt." Her sobs start again.

"Elli," Reese says, moving closer and kneeling down to be at her level. "Why don't you let your dad get you cleaned up, and then you and I can go back to the house and I'll paint your nails for you while we wait on everyone else to get back? Like a mini spa day."

Elli looks at Reese, tears still running down her cheeks. "I don't want it to hurt," she whimpers.

"I know," Reese says, holding her hands out. "It might sting for a second, but we have to get all the dirt out. Otherwise, it can get infected. Then it will really hurt."

Elli puts her hands in Reese's and closes her eyes. "Okay, but hurry." She holds her breath.

Reese runs her thumb across the side of Elli's hand, and I bite back a smile. Seeing her comfort my girl is doing funny things to my heart.

Carefully, I pour a bit of water over her hands, washing away the dirt that is on the surface. "It looks like the scratches aren't too deep. I bet by tomorrow, they'll all feel better."

"I hope so," Elli says tearfully.

Once I have her palms patted dry, I apply antibiotic ointment and bandages to the deeper scratches, one on each palm. I wipe away her tears and kiss her cheek. "Are you sure you want to head back?" I ask. "You were having fun before you fell."

She nods her head. "I'm sure."

Reese stands and wipes her hands on her shorts before placing a hand on Elli's shoulder.

I put everything back in the backpack and stand. "All right, we'll go back."

Elli looks to Reese, then back to me. "Can I go back with Ms. Reese?"

My heart squeezes in my chest. My little girl is hurt, and she doesn't want me. "Uh, sure. If Ms. Reese is good with that."

"Yep." She smiles and takes Elli's elbow, careful to avoid her scraped hands. "I've got this."

"Okay," I say, still feeling unsettled. "You can give her one of the junior ibuprofens in the medicine kit if she's still hurting when you get back to the house."

She nods at me and pats Elli's back. "We'll be fine."

"Bye, Elli," Liam says sadly from beside his mom. "I hope it doesn't hurt anymore."

"Keep looking for one," Elli says before waving and walking off with Reese back towards the trail head.

"Looking for what?" Morgan asks Liam.

He shrugs. "A wishing flower."

"What are you two wishing for?"

"It's a secret," Liam says and grins.

I smile at that and glance back in time to see Elli and Reese turn the corner out of sight.

My heart stutters, and I grin. I wonder if I should make a wish of my own.

CHAPTER FOURTEEN

Reese

"HOW ARE YOU FEELING?" I ask Elli as we approach the house. "Any better?" Her tears stopped shortly after we started back, but she's been pretty quiet.

"Yeah." She sniffles. "My knees hurt."

I open the door and motion her in. "Have a seat at the table. I'll go grab the medicine." I leave her sitting in the dining area and get the tote with the medicine off the top of the fridge. Setting it on the counter, I find the junior pain relievers, and shake one out for her.

I grab a juice box from the fridge and set it down in front of her before handing her the little orange pill. "This should help."

She chews it up and drinks the juice quickly. "Ugh," she groans. "Those are so yucky."

I laugh. "You're not wrong. I don't like medicine much myself."

"Can I go put on some shorts? These pants are all dirty."

"Of course, I'll go get the nail supplies and meet you back here, okay?" I watch as Elli hops down from the chair and slowly shuffles toward her room to change. Poor thing. It's never fun to get hurt, especially on vacation, and even worse when it's in front of your friends.

I quickly head to my room to grab the nail kit I packed. Doing my nails is one way I take some time for myself. Self care is important, or so they say. Especially when I spend my days surrounded by preschoolers.

"All right," I say, setting everything down on the table in front of Elli. "You beat me back to the table."

"I hurried," she says, excitedly looking at the small pile on the table.

"I have pink or lavender. Which color do you want?" I set them both in front of her so she can make her choice.

"Can I have both?" she asks.

"Of course, let's do most of your fingers one color, and have an accent nail. How does that sound?" I wiggle my fingers for her to see. My nails are bright pink with one white nail on each hand.

"Perfect." She grins and settles back in her chair.

I'm grateful getting a mini manicure is taking her mind off her hurt knees. I grab a few paper towels and place her hands on top so we don't make a mess. Grabbing the nail file, I get started on the edges of her nails. "Do you enjoy getting your nails painted?"

Elli giggles when I file close to the edge of her pinky. "I never had my nails painted before, so I don't know."

I pause, surprised Heather hasn't ever painted her nails. "Oh," I say, unsure how to proceed. "By the time I was eight, my mom was hiding her polish, so I'd stay out of it." I laugh to lighten the mood.

The truth was, my mother was so embarrassed when I came home from school with red nails in the third grade that she banned me from polishing them again until I was a teenager. "Red is not a color for little girls," she said angrily before sitting me down and removing every bit of polish from my fingers and toes. I cried. Not understanding why I couldn't wear red. She wore red, and it was beautiful.

"My mommy doesn't paint her nails either." She shrugs and smiles. "I'm excited."

I hesitate. I wonder if Heather will be upset that Elli got her nails painted. Daniel would have nixed the idea if he didn't approve, I'm sure, but I'm suddenly uneasy. I definitely don't want to step on anyone's toes.

I sigh, in for a penny, in for a pound. I'll just have to hope Heather isn't very upset.

Elli decides her pointer fingers will be pink, and the rest the light purple. I've just painted her last nail when everyone walks in.

"Hey!" Elli shouts. "Come see my nails!" She holds her hands up and wiggles her fingers. "I even have an accent nail."

Liam sprints into the room, sliding to a stop in front of Elli. "Be careful," she says, pulling her knees under the table.

"Sorry," Liam says sheepishly. "Can I see?"

Elli holds out her nails for everyone to inspect.

"They're beautiful, Elli girl," Daniel says, smiling warmly. "How are you feeling?"

"I'm okay," she looks down at her knees. "I think I've got a bruise."

Daniel crouches down and looks at her knees, which are red and mottled from her fall. "Yep, you sure do." He gently plants a kiss on each one, making my heart trip in my chest. "Did that help?"

"Dad." Elli draws his name out on an exasperated sigh. "You know that doesn't really help, right?"

Daniel's hands shoot to his heart. "What?" he says, pretending to be shocked. "How did I not know that? All these years . . ." he says, shaking his head.

Elli giggles. "Do you think we could call Mommy and show her my nails?"

"Of course." Daniel helps her down from the chair. "Let's go to the deck and you can show her the view, too."

He hands her his phone, and slides open the door. He stops beside me and smiles. "Thank you."

I nod. "You're welcome. We had fun. I hope Heather doesn't get mad about the nails. Elli said she's never had them painted before."

"Nah," Daniel says confidently. "She won't care." Then he steps outside and closes the door.

I watch as he scoots in next to her on the lounge chair. They really have a special bond.

"That was nice of you," Morgan says.

I jump. I didn't hear her come into the dining area. "Eh, I loved nail polish when I was her age. I figured it might cheer her up."

"Looks like you were right." Morgan points out the window.

Elli is holding her fingers up in front of the phone and laughing.

I stand and grab the nail kit. "I'll put this back in my room and help you get dinner started."

Morgan nods and moves to the kitchen. "That would be great. Thanks. We're having tacos tonight."

Once I'm back in the kitchen, I stop to wash my hands, and then cut the veggies for the taco toppings.

"Can I ask you something?"

"Of course." Morgan stops stirring the meat and turns to me. "Ask away."

"Well . . ." I pause, unsure how to ask. "When you met Brant, how did you know it was going to work out?"

Morgan stirs the meat again, turning off the burner and moving to the sink to drain off the fat. "Honestly, I didn't." She shakes the strainer and dumps the meat back into the skillet. "I was scared. I'd already loved and lost, and didn't want to get my heart broken again."

I nod. "I can understand that. But you gave it a go, anyway. Why?"

Morgan dumps the seasoning and water into the skillet and stirs, taking her time to answer. "Somehow, without me even realizing it, Brant had gotten under my skin. I thought about him constantly. When we were in the same room, my eyes always found his."

I inhale deeply and let my breath out slowly, willing my eyes not to search him out.

"I tried ignoring it, shutting him out, and, as you know, I was miserable. Susan told me to take a chance, and Brant was so patient while I figured it out."

"I remember that," I say. "You were pretty miserable when you shut him out. I've seen you blossom since you started dating him. It's like his love helped you bloom again."

Morgan nods. "I had to let go of the plan I had for my life when William died. Then I had to do it again when I let Brant in. Love is a feeling, but even more so, it's a choice, an action. That's not something you can plan. Not really."

"Was it worth it?" I ask hesitantly. "Taking the risk and letting him in?"

Morgan's eyes take on a dreamy quality. "It was definitely worth it."

I think about that while I finish getting the avocado and tomatoes ready. We finish getting dinner ready, and set everything out buffet style on the counter before calling everyone in to eat.

I stand back, leaning against the counter as everyone else gets their food. The gentle teasing, laughter, and smiles are not what I'm used to at gatherings. My parents were always so determined to appear to be the perfect family, we rarely had genuine fun. Daniel's laugh catches my attention and pulls me out of my thoughts. My eyes find his, crinkled with laughter, and something clicks into place.

This—I want this. Genuine joy, and a man who has fun with his family. I want vacations filled with laughter and teasing, friends and happiness. I want nights playing games around the table. For the first time, my idea of suitable feels different.

Daniel winks at me, and heat blooms from my chest down to my toes.

I think I want him.

I give myself a mental shake. Even if I wanted to explore the pull I feel, it's impossible. He's given no indication that he feels more than friendship. I can't risk making a fool of myself in front of everyone, only to be turned down. That would be incredibly awkward. I'm enjoying this time with these people far too much to mess it up.

I push off the counter and fix my dinner.

"About time," Evan groans. "I was holding back on seconds until you got some food. I'm still hungry." He rubs his flat stomach as if to show how starved he is.

"You already ate a ton, Ev. I doubt you'll starve to death if you don't get more food." Brant shakes his head and throws a wadded napkin at him.

Evan ducks. "I'm a growing boy," he says, grinning. "I need my fuel."

Liam looks down at his food, then back at Evan. "How much do I need to eat to grow big like you?"

The table erupts into laughter. Morgan is wiping her eyes with a napkin when Evan finally calms down enough to respond. "You'll get there. It takes time and fuel. You just eat till you're full. You're growing at the perfect speed."

Liam's shoulders slump, the creases between his eyebrows disappearing. "Thank goodness," he whispers. "I don't think I could eat as much as him," he says to Elli.

Elli covers her mouth with her hand and giggles. "I don't think anyone could eat as much as Mr. Evan," she chokes out.

Evan's hand goes to his heart in mock hurt. "Little girl, you wound me."

After a few more giggles, everyone settles back into the conversation. Evan has piled his plate high for a second time, causing Liam's eyes to bulge out like a goldfish.

"Why don't you kids go play outside for a bit while we clean up?" Morgan asks, standing.

Daniel stands and starts clearing the table. "We've got it tonight." He nods his head at the guys, but he's looking at Morgan . . . and me. "You cooked, we'll clean. Why don't you join the kids outside and just relax?"

"Perfect." Morgan grins and grabs my arm, guiding me to the sliding glass door and out onto the porch. My eyes never leave his. There's that longing again, and I'm finding it harder to ignore.

CHAPTER FIFTEEN

Daniel

"YOU GONNA KEEP STARING at her all night, or help us clean up?" Evan asks, bumping into me.

"What?" I break eye contact, and take a deep breath. "I wasn't staring," I claim.

Brant chuckles. "Sure, whatever you say."

I grab the stack of dishes I'd been collecting, and turn toward the kitchen. Setting them into the sink, I start the water and open the dishwasher. "I wasn't staring," I insist.

My declaration is met with an unusual silence. I stop rinsing dishes and turn to face my two best friends. "You're never quiet," I state, waiting for one of them to speak. They are looking at each other, speaking with raised eyebrows and head nods. "Spit it out," I grunt.

Brant sighs. "You like her."

I'm shaking my head before he even finishes the sentence. "She's friendly, and she's Morgan's friend. That's it."

"No, you *like* her," Evan says sternly. "You liked her at Brant's wedding, and you like her even more now. You think we haven't noticed how you can't keep your eyes off of her?"

I turn and start rinsing dishes, putting them into the dishwasher. "Even if I did like her, which I'm not saying I do—but even if I did, she's not interested in someone a decade older than her." I pause. Not facing them makes it easier to get this out. "Plus, I'm not up for getting my heart broken again."

Evan steps up and turns off the water as I load the last dish. "Dude, have you not seen how she looks at you? She blushes every time you say something to her."

I look out onto the back deck, where Morgan and Reese are deep in conversation. Elli and Liam run by kicking a ball around the back yard. What if she did like me too? A warmth spreads through my chest and causes my breath to shudder.

"Heather wasn't the right one for you, man." Brant pats me on the shoulder. "She didn't want the same things as you. Could you ever see her here, vacationing at the lake?"

I pause and imagine Heather here. She'd be miserable. She was more of a fancy hotel and facials girl. "I know," I say softly. "I knew we weren't right for each other before we even said 'I do', but we'd been together for so long, and I thought we'd figure it out. Every marriage takes compromise, right?"

"Yes," Brant says slowly. "Every marriage is work. It takes communication, compromise, and love to make it through. Both people have to want to work toward the same ultimate goals."

I nod my head. "That's where we went wrong. I wanted a simple life," I say, my hand sweeping out toward the picturesque lake through the windows. "Heather wanted to *be* something. At first I thought we could both get what we wanted, but it turned out we just couldn't get on the same page."

There was more to it, of course, but that's what it ultimately came down to. We were just too different. Our goals were too far apart.

"From what I've seen of Reese, she isn't looking to lead some fancy life. She seems to hate being the center of attention. Morgan said she hasn't ever seen Reese as relaxed as she's been here at the lake." Brant smiles at me. "From where I stand, it looks like the two of you have a lot in common."

"And enough chemistry to start the bonfire," Evan pipes in. "Just think about it. If you like her as much as I think you do, do you really want to sit by when she brings someone else on vacation next summer?"

A burning in my gut takes me by surprise.

Evan laughs. "By the look on your face, I'd say that is a no. Then, what are you waiting for?"

I stuff my hands in my pockets. "What are you doing giving out dating advice? Aren't you the one who swears he isn't settling down?"

Evan grins. "Yeah, but that's because I haven't found anyone who makes me love drunk." He reaches into the fridge and grabs a bottle of water. "You, my friend, are love drunk." He points the bottle at me and heads outside with the girls.

I stand there, hands in my pockets, unsure what to do. Of course I like her. She is gorgeous, funny, kind, great with Elli. What's not to like? I just don't know what to do about it.

The next morning, I'm in the kitchen making pancakes when everyone makes their way into the living area.

"What are you doing up so early?" Evan asks, stretching his arms above his head and yawning.

I point the spatula at him. "You, sir, snore. You should really get that checked. It can't be healthy." I shake my head, stifling a yawn.

"I don't snore," Evan says defensively.

"Yeah, you do." Brant says on his way to the coffee pot. "Everyone in the house can hear you."

"I'm going to check on Mittens," Evan says, snagging his phone off the counter and heading to the back porch.

I shake my head. There's something going on with the neighbor. I just wonder if she's the one who's going to knock Evan's socks off.

I finish plating the pancakes and take the overflowing platter to the table. "Breakfast is served."

I already put out fruit and juice, so everyone sits and starts piling their plates full.

"What do you guys want to do today?" Morgan asks while cutting up Liam's pancake.

Liam and Elli share a look, and Elli shakes her head no. Hmm, wonder what that was all about.

"Can we go swimming?" Liam asks, stuffing a big bite into his mouth.

An hour later, the guys have the kids in the lake splashing around. The girls are taking forever to get ready.

Brant stops, Liam high in his arms, ready to be tossed, and stares back toward the house. "Something wrong?" I ask, turning to check what he is staring at. The breath is punched from my lungs. Reese's red hair is braided and hangs over a bare shoulder. The modest one-piece suit has just one thick shoulder strap. She is gorgeous.

"Don't swallow your tongue," Evan jokes and splashes water into my face.

I splash him back, and soon everyone is splashing and giggling. Reese and Morgan wade in and join in the fun.

"When are you going to ask her out already?" Evan asks the next evening.

I'm saved from having to give it too much more thought when Elli comes running inside, Liam hot on her trail. "Daddy, can we go fishing?"

After lunch yesterday, it rained, so we stayed inside and played games. It was a nice way to pass the time, but I'm thankful for the better weather today. Too much time inside with Reese in close proximity has me wishing for things I shouldn't.

Glad for something else to do, I jump on it. "Sounds great. Let's grab the gear out of the shed."

"Are you good with both kids? I'd like to take Morgan back out on the lake to watch the sunset."

I nod. "Of course." I reach into the freezer and grab the package of frozen bait shrimp we brought with us. "I've got them. You and Morgan enjoy the sunset."

Brant grins and slaps my shoulder. "Thanks, man."

Elli, Liam, and I make our way down to the shed to grab the fishing supplies. Brant is talking to Morgan on the deck. I grin when she jumps up and hugs him. They really are a great couple. My eyes slide over to Reese, and my chest aches. Fishing. Focus on fishing.

The kids have already picked out their poles, when I find the tackle box and grab a pole for myself. We pass Brant and Morgan on their way to grab the canoe and wave. I find a spot closer to the trailhead and settle everything on the ground. "Do you guys remember how to bait your hooks?"

Liam scrunches his face. "I don't like it."

Soft laughter makes me spin toward the shed. Reese is walking our way, fishing pole in hand. "I don't either," she says to Liam. "But I do like to fish." She looks at me and smiles. "Maybe Mr. Daniel wouldn't mind baiting our hooks?"

She bats her eyelashes and I can't help but laugh. "Baiting your hook is part of the fun," I say, shaking my head. "Besides, it's frozen shrimp, not wiggly worms," I say, reaching over and tickling Elli. She hates fishing with worms, too.

"I don't like wiggly worms, so my daddy always gets the frozen stuff." She grins. "It's a lot easier, and way less gross."

Liam looks relieved. Reese, on the other hand . . . She still looks uncertain.

"Try it. If it's as bad as you think it will be, then I'll bait your hooks."

A few minutes later, everyone has baited their own hooks and cast their lines. "How was it?" I ask.

Liam grins up at me. "Way better than the wiggle worms Daddy uses."

I still can't get over how sweet it is to hear him call Brant "Daddy." When Elli called me Dada for the first time, my heart almost burst from my chest. I'd never been so happy in all my life. There's nothing like being someone's daddy.

"I'm glad. What about you, Reese? Frozen shrimp as bad as wiggly worms?"

Elli giggles, and Reese grins at her. "Nope, that was a million times better!"

I nod my head and focus on my line. A few seconds later, Elli squeals.

"Daddy," she calls. "I think I got something!"

I look at her pole, dipping and pulling. "You've definitely got something there, nice and easy, remember?"

She nods, her eyes focused on her line.

"Slowly try to reel it in. Not too fast, now. Patient." I set my pole down and stand behind her for support. "That's it, you've got it."

Elli finally pulls in the fish, a little smallmouth bass. "I did it!" she shouts, jumping up and down.

"You certainly did," I say, grabbing the fish and unhooking it. "Want to throw it back?"

"Yes!" Elli carefully grabs the fish and lets it go back into the water. "I did it all by myself," she squeals.

"Way to go!" Reese says, stepping in and giving her a high five. "You caught the first fish of the night, too!"

We stand at the shoreline fishing for another hour or so. Each of the kids has caught several fish. I've spent more time helping them than I have actually fishing, but I enjoy it. These are memories I hope Elli cherishes.

"I've got one!" Reese says, her pole really pulling. "It feels like it's huge."

She giggles, and the sound goes straight to my gut. She looks so beautiful, arching back with her pole, her hair shining in the sunset's light. "Keep pulling it in," I say, going to stand beside her for backup. "You've got it."

She struggles for a few minutes, but manages fine on her own. "Whoa!" Liam says as the fish finally hits the shore. "It's huge!"

Reese is laughing and clapping her hands, excitement oozing out of her. "I did it!" she exclaims, and jumps into my arms. I catch her and grin. "I caught one all by myself!"

Holding her in my arms feels good—too good—but before I can set her down, my lips have found hers. Fireworks erupt behind my eyelids, and heat slams into my body. She kisses me back, and it's heaven. I'm lost in the scent of her, the feel of her . . . until I hear giggles, and I'm brought back to reality.

"Um, Daddy . . ." Elli giggles. "Are you going to kiss Ms. Reese like that all night, or are you going to put the fish back?"

Reese slides out of my arms and looks to her feet. "Oh, my gosh," she whispers. "I'm so sorry." She quickly grabs the fish, unhooks it, and tosses it back into the water.

If the kiss didn't rock my world, her making quick work of sending the bass back into the lake did. Elli and Liam are standing with heads together, whispering and giggling.

"Time to pack it up, guys," I say, shaking myself into action. "Let's get everything back in the shed for the night."

Liam and Elli make short work of collecting their poles, and head to the shed, leaving Reese and me behind.

"I'm sorry," Reese says. "I wasn't thinking."

Even in the setting sunlight, I can tell she's blushing. "No," I whisper. "I'm sorry for kissing you like that. I shouldn't have put you on the spot."

Her eyes snap up to me, and she rubs her lips together. "Oh."

"Reese," I say, hesitant to say more. "That kiss . . ."

"It's okay," she says, grabbing her pole and turning back toward the shed. "I know you didn't mean it."

What? I gently reach out for her arm, and turn her to face me. "That's not what I was going to say, Red."

"It's not?" she asks in a breathy whisper.

"No," I say softly, stepping a bit closer. "I was going to say that was the best kiss of my life, and even though I know I shouldn't, I can't help but want to do it again."

Her eyes go wide with my admission. "You do?"

I nod, letting her absorb my words. "I do. I've wanted to kiss you since I saw you at Brant and Morgan's wedding."

She swallows audibly. "You have?"

I chuckle. "I have, but I didn't think you'd be interested. I'm a man with baggage, and I'm sure I'm not the type of man you're looking for." I rub my hand down her arm before letting go and stepping back.

"You deserve everything Reese."

She stands in the same position, unmoving. Staring at me. The tension is so thick, I'm sure Evan can feel it from his spot on the deck. He's spent the evening on the deck talking on the phone. To whom, I have no idea, but if I had to guess, I'd put my money on a certain cat sitter.

Chapter Sixteen

Reese

I STAND FROZEN IN place, my lips still tingling from the kiss. He's wanted to kiss me since the wedding?

"Hey," Morgan says, stepping out of the canoe. "What are you doing standing down here by yourself?"

Her voice startles me, and I jump a bit. "We were just fishing," I say a little too loudly.

"Okay . . ." she draws out. She glances to the porch and back to me. "Why is everyone else up there, and you're down here?"

I glance to the porch where Liam has his hands stretched out, presumably to show Evan how big his fish was. Turning back, I see Brant taking the canoe back to the shed.

"How was your sunset on the lake?" I ask, hoping she will let the change of subject slide.

Morgan's eyebrow shoots up, like it does when one of our students is trying to get out of trouble. "Reese, are you okay?"

I laugh—a strangled sound, even to my own ears. "Yes, of course. Don't be silly." I wave my hand frantically in front of myself.

"Are the mosquitoes out tonight?" Brant calls from across the yard.

I drop my head and laugh. "No."

"Um, okay then." He shakes his head and continues toward the house.

Morgan pins me with her "spill it" stare, and the words tumble out before I can catch them. "I just had the best kiss of my life, and I don't know what to do next."

Morgan's brows shoot so high, they disappear behind her bangs. Her head whips to the back porch, mouth dropped open.

"Morgan," I whisper. "Don't stare like that. They'll know!"

"What?" Her head whips around so fast I'm afraid she'll give herself whiplash. "What do you mean 'they'll know?' Morgan, who'd you kiss?"

I rub my hands on my pants, not willing to get fish slime on my new shirt, but needing the feeling to ground myself. "Daniel," I whisper.

"It's about time," Morgan says, laughing.

"What?" This time it's my head that snaps up too quickly. "What do you mean?"

She laughs and takes my arm, walking me to the fire pit where several chairs are set out in a circle. "Brant and I noticed a spark between you two at the wedding. Neither one of you could stop finding the other in the crowd. That spark has obviously grown as you've spent more time together."

"Um," I stammer, unsure what to say. "And you guys are okay with that?"

"Honey, all we want is for our friends to be happy. If you find happiness with each other, that's great." Morgan leans back in the chair and crosses her legs in front of her. "If not . . ." she shrugs.

"I never thought I'd be attracted to someone older than me. My mom would flip if she found out. Especially since he has a kid." I sigh.

"Let me ask you something," Morgan says softly. "Do you like him?"

My eyes find him, and warmth spreads throughout my body. "More than I've ever liked anyone in my life."

She nods. "Does it bother you that he has a daughter?"

I pause and let her question roll around in my head. "No," I say honestly. "He is a fantastic father and seems to have a good relationship with his ex." I cringe.

"That bothers you. Why?"

I sigh and scoot further back into the chair. "I'm not sure," I say, softly. "I guess I just don't want to feel like second best. All my life, I've never felt good enough. I was always too loud, too embarrassing, too ... me." I fidget with my fingers and take a breath. "Heather is so put together, and I'm just ... not. I don't want to always be worried about saying or doing the right thing. It's exhausting."

Morgan nods, waiting for me to go on.

"I could never compete with her."

"There's no competition," a deep voice says.

I gasp and bury my face in my hands—good thing I wiped them on my shorts. Please, let me just disappear right now.

I hear Morgan shift in her chair. "I'm going inside to get the kids ready for bed." She puts her hand on my shoulder and whispers to me, "You're enough, just the way you are."

Tears prick the corners of my eyes. This is not how I saw this trip going.

My heart races as Daniel scoots a chair closer to me. He leans over and gently pulls my hands from my face.

"Hey," he says softly. "I thought we could talk about the kiss. I had no idea you were feeling so conflicted."

I tip my head back and take a deep breath. Holding it for a few seconds before slowly letting it go. "It's okay."

He takes my hand in his, and rubs his thumb over my knuckles. "Heather and I weren't good for each other. I think we both knew it, but we didn't know how to let go." He sighs. "When Elli came along, I doubled down, hoping that we could figure it out."

"You don't ..." I start, but he cuts me off.

"I want to talk about this," he says, squeezing my hand gently. "Obviously, it didn't work. My heart was broken, but not for the reason you may think. I was disappointed that the ideal—what we could have been—was gone, and shattered that I'd have to split time with Elli girl."

The tears I've been struggling to hold back slip down my face. "I'm so sorry," I say.

He glances at me, and his lips lift in a half smile. "Sometimes, our best laid plans aren't meant to be. I haven't been interested in someone since the divorce. I always thought I'd be better off alone. Just me and Elli."

I nod in understanding. "I get it."

He waits for me to find his eyes again to speak. "I don't think you do," he says, leaning closer. "I can't stop thinking about you. Believe me, I've tried. I've told myself all the reasons I should leave you alone, and yet, I can't. I'm drawn to you in a way I can't explain. I've never felt this way before."

I suck in a breath and tuck my shaking hands beneath my legs. "I feel the same way."

Daniel grins, the corners of his eyes crinkling in the way I love.

"I'd really like to take you on a date when we get back. If you'd like that. No pressure."

I nod, my body feeling as though it could float off this chair. "I'd love that."

The sliding glass door slides open, causing us both to jump. Daniel laughs as Elli bounds down the steps of the porch and across the grass.

"Night, Daddy. Ms. Reese." She leans in and gives Daniel a hug. "Is Ms. Reese your girlfriend now?"

Bless her heart, she tried to whisper, but it came out as an excited shout. Daniel glances at me and grins. "Well, I haven't asked her yet," he says conspiratorially.

Elli shifts and puts her little hand on her hip. "Well, what are you waiting for? You already kissed her. That means she should be your girlfriend, right?" she asks.

I laugh and reach out for her. "Do I get a hug goodnight, too?"

She grins but doesn't move. "Not till my daddy asks you to be his girlfriend." She shoots him an annoyed glance.

"I might want to ask her in private, you know," Daniel says, chuckling.

She shakes her little head. "Well, it's too late now," she says, grinning. "Don't you want her to be your girlfriend? She likes to fish, and paints nails—what more could you want?"

Morgan's laughter bursts into the night air. "Elli, say goodnight and leave your daddy alone," she calls.

"Ugh," Elli sighs. "Fine." She leans in and gives me a hug. "Goodnight, Ms. Reese. I hope you're my daddy's girlfriend tomorrow."

My heart is gone. It's now in the hands of this adorable little girl. "Me too," I whisper, my eyes on Daniel's. "Me too."

CHAPTER SEVENTEEN

Daniel

ELLI SKIPS OFF TO the house, and I can't help but grin. The fact that she wants Reese and I to be together only confirms that this is the right move. "So," I pause, waiting for Reese to make eye contact with me. "How would you feel about making it official? I know it may seem sudden, but I feel like we've gotten to know each other pretty well over the last few weeks." I pause, ready to continue listing all the reasons she should be mine.

"Daniel," she says, reaching out and touching my arm. "I would love to make it official. If our 'official' dates are half as much fun as the times we've spent together so far, I can't wait to see what the future holds."

Unable to resist, I pull her into my arms and place a soft kiss on her lips. "Thank you," I whisper.

The next morning, I wake up to Elli bouncing on my bed.

"Did you ask her, Daddy?" She giggles when I grab her legs and pull her down.

"I did," I say, unable to hide my smile.

"Did she say yes? Is she going to be your girlfriend?" Elli holds her breath and waits for the answer.

I nod. "She is. How do you feel about that?"

Elli lets out a squeal so loud, I'm sure she woke the neighbors. "I'm going to have a bonus mom!"

"Whoa!" I say, tickling her. "Too soon, Elli girl."

She just grins and launches herself from the bed. "I have to go tell Liam!"

I laugh as she dashes out the door, slamming it behind her. Rolling over, I glance at the alarm clock on the nightstand. Six am—good grief. Why can't she wake up that excited on the days I have to work? Groaning, I push myself into a sitting position and stretch my arms above my head. I wonder if Brant and Morgan would mind watching Elli for a while. I have a girlfriend to woo.

The smell of coffee brewing makes the early morning bearable. "Good morning," I say to Brant and Morgan when I enter the kitchen. "How would you two feel about keeping an eye on Elli today?"

Brant grins. "I don't think that would be a problem. Big plans?"

I shrug. "Still deciding on exactly what to do, but yeah. I'd like to spend the day with Reese."

"That's a great idea," Morgan says. She hands me a mug of coffee. "What are you thinking? Maybe we can help you plan."

Thirty minutes later, we've come up with a day I hope Reese will never forget.

"What are you guys discussing so intently this morning?" Reese asks. She grabs a mug and fills it with coffee. "It's too early to be so serious."

I laugh. "Good morning, Red. Did you sleep okay?"

She grunts. "You know, mornings come too early when you stayed up late the night before with your boyfriend." She grins at me and winks. "Worth it."

"I'm glad you think so," I say winking back. "Can you be ready to go in about an hour? I've got a surprise planned."

Reese looks from me to Morgan, then to Brant and back to me. "A surprise?"

"Don't look so shocked." I laugh. "A surprise. Can you be ready?"

"What about Elli?" she asks and my heart melts for her a little more.

"We've got Elli and Liam today," Brant says. "We're going to fill up the water balloons and let them chase Evan around."

"Hey!" Evan calls out from the hallway. "I heard that."

Everyone bursts out laughing.

"So, where are we going?" Reese asks.

I glance over at her in the passenger seat of my truck. She looks beautiful in her cut off shorts, light blue tank, and her hair pulled up into a messy bun—casual, relaxed. "You'll just have to wait and see."

I have to admit, I'm kind of enjoying keeping her in the dark for a bit. I just hope she likes what I've planned.

When we finally pull into the gravel area designated for parking, Reese turns in her seat and shrieks. "Seriously?"

I hesitate. Maybe this wasn't a good idea. "Well, we don't have to," I say. " I just…"

"Are you kidding me? Yes, we do! This is so exciting! I've never been ziplining before, but I've always wanted to try it!" She unbuckles her seat belt and hops out of the truck. "Are you coming!"

Relief floods my body. Thank goodness. "You bet," I say smiling ear to ear.

After getting us checked in, the young man behind the desks points us to an area labeled "Safety Training." There's a short video before our guide, another young man in cargo pants and a polo, comes to collect us.

"Welcome to Zipline Adventures, I'm Tommy. I'll be your guide today. Have you ever been ziplining before?" He leads us to an area that has safety harnesses and helmets already laid out.

"Nope," we say in unison.

Tommy laughs. "I see. Well, as long as you follow the safety instructions, you two should be fine."

A few minutes later, we are fitted in our harnesses and safety gear. Tommy has given us another run down of the safety protocols, and my stomach feels like it might explode from nerves.

"You okay?" Reese whispers as Tommy leads us up the trail to the start of the zipline.

"Yeah, just nervous." I whisper back. "I'll be fine." I grin at her and give her arm a soft squeeze.

At the top of the trail, Tommy pauses and points behind us. "Take a look," he says.

Turning, I'm stunned. The view is breathtaking. The sun is shining on the green trees that grow along the mountainside.

"It's gorgeous," Reese says quietly.

I take her hand. "It is," I agree. The view, and the woman beside me.

"Alright, who's going first?" Tommy asks, stepping onto the platform.

"I guess I'll go first," I say stepping up. Tommy connects me to the line and calls across a walkie talkie to the guide waiting on the other side.

"When I count to three, step off the ledge."

Tommy starts the count down, and on three, I step off and let go. My stomach drops into my toes for a moment, as the wind starts to rush past my face. I realize I'm holding my breath and force myself to exhale. The view is amazing. I throw my arms wide, enjoying the feeling of freedom. No wonder people enjoy this, it's a huge rush. Too soon, I'm coming to the landing platform where another guide is waiting to help me off the line.

"Well, how was it?" he asks, helping me find my footing.

"Amazing!" I chuckle. "I've never experienced anything like it."

He calls over to let Tommy know the line is free, and a few minutes later, a grinning Reese joins me on the landing platform.

"That was the most intense thing I've ever done!" She giggles. "I definitely want to do this again sometime."

The landing guide, Becker, guides us back to the safety area and collects our gear.

"Seriously," Reese says grinning. "Best date ever!"

She leans in and kisses me, taking my breath away. "I agree, but it's not over yet."

"It's not?"

"Nope." I take her hand and guide her back to the truck. "Ready for part two?"

CHAPTER EIGHTEEN

Reese

"I HOPE YOU'RE HUNGRY," Daniel says. He pulls into the parking lot of an older building with a rustic sign out front that says, "Ma's Diner."

"Starving actually." My stomach chooses that moment to growl loudly. "Apparently ziplining takes it out of you."

Daniel chuckles and rubs his stomach. "I guess so, I'm pretty hungry myself."

Ma's Diner is a cute little diner with a walk-up counter. After we order, we grab our tray and head for a table on the back patio overlooking the lake.

"Thank you for this," I say, gesturing around us.

"Thank you," Daniel says taking my hand across the table. "This may seem weird, but it feels like we have been dating for weeks already. I really like spending time with you. With Elli, and alone."

Butterflies battle for space in my chest. "I agree," I say softly.

We spend the afternoon visiting the little shops in downtown before heading back to the lake house. When we pull into the driveway, Morgan is waiting on the porch with a picnic basket in her hands.

"Thanks," Daniel says, grabbing the basket and giving Morgan a quick hug. "How's Elli?"

"She's great, don't you worry about her." Morgan waves in my direction. "Now scoot before those two come find you and convince you to take them along."

"Take them along where?" I ask, confused.

"Come on," Daniel says, reaching for my elbow. "I've got one more surprise in store for you."

He leads me to the back of the house where Brant has a canoe already in the water. "Have fun," he says, winking at me. He pats Daniel on the shoulder and turns heading back to the house.

"I thought we'd end the evening with a sunset on the water. How does that sound?" Daniel looks unsure of himself.

"It sounds like the perfect way to end a perfect date." I say and step into the canoe.

This week at the lake has been the most relaxing time of my life, and I'm not ready for it to end. Today, it's back to reality, though. The cabin is all packed up, and we're just finishing loading the cars.

"Daddy, can Reese ride with us?" Elli asks, pulling on Daniel's shirt.

"Of course," he says, grinning. "If she would like to."

The way he defers to what I may want makes my heart sing. No one has ever given as much care to what I'd like. "I'd love to," I say, grinning at them both.

"Great," Daniel says, going to get my bag from the back of Brant's truck.

"You could leave it there," I call. "My car is parked at their house."

He turns and shakes his head. "You may need something on the way back."

A few minutes later, we've all said goodbye and Daniel has put my bag in the back of his truck. Elli is settled in the back seat, her head bobbing along with the music playing on the radio. Daniel slides into the driver's seat beside me and smiles. "Ready?" he asks, buckling his seat belt.

"Ready."

The drive passes with Elli recounting all her favorite moments of our trip. Including, much to my shock, the kiss Daniel and I shared at the lake. "I can't wait to tell Mommy," she says, laughing.

I stiffen in the seat. Daniel grabs my hand and gives it a squeeze. "Well, let me tell Grandma, okay?"

Elli sighs. "Fine."

Daniel laughs. "Elli has a habit of sharing information before I'm ready for her to. She's already told my mom all about you."

My eyes go wide, and I suck in a breath. "What? How?"

"My daddy liked you at Mr. Brant's wedding. I knew it. He kept getting goo-goo eyes."

Daniel laughs. "Thanks, kid."

I blush and smile at Daniel.

Before I know it, we are pulling into Brant's driveway behind my car. "Thank you for inviting me to ride with you."

"You're welcome," Elli calls from behind me.

"See you later," I say, stepping out of the truck. I meet Daniel at the back where he is holding my bag.

"I'm not ready to let you go," Daniel says softly. "Can we swing by your place with pizza and a movie?"

I grin. "I'd love that. Give me about an hour to unpack and shower?"

He nods. "Sounds perfect," he says, bringing my hand to his lips and giving it a soft kiss. "What's your address?"

I rattle off my address and give him a hug.

"See you soon," he whispers into my ear before pulling back.

I nod and float on air to my car.

While I drive home, I keep bursting with giddy laughter. I debate calling Anne, but I decide this calls for an in-person discussion. Besides, I haven't turned my phone on yet, holding onto the last bit of the break.

I pull into my parking spot and turn the car off. Not quite ready to head inside, I sit for a second, my head tipped back, and bask in the joy I'm feeling. I can't remember a time I've felt so happy. So free to be myself.

I hop out of the car and grab my bag, rushing to get inside and get settled before Daniel and Elli come over for dinner. I can't remember what state my apartment was in when I left. I'm not always the neatest when I'm packing for a trip.

I step inside my apartment and freeze.

"Well, there you are. I've been waiting for hours."

CHAPTER NINETEEN

Daniel

"How do you feel about a movie and pizza with Reese tonight?" I ask once we are on the road back home.

"I love it," Elli says before yawning. "Can I wear my pajamas?"

I laugh. "You bet."

A few minutes later, I'm pulling into the driveway behind Heather's car. I didn't expect her back yet.

"Hey," she says as I step out of the truck. "I know I wasn't due back until next weekend, but we wrapped up early, and I missed Elli."

"MOM!" Elli shouts as she runs around the front of the truck. "You're back!" Elli's little body slams into Heather, almost knocking her down. I reach out a hand and steady her.

"Seems like she missed you too," I say, laughing.

"Mom! Look, you can see my nails in person now. Aren't they pretty?" Elli shoves her hands in her mom's face. "Reese painted them. We went fishing and caught a fish, and Daddy kissed Reese, and now she's his girlfriend." Elli sucks in a breath. "We had so much fun!"

Heather laughs and hugs Elli. "You must've had fun," she says, laughing. "And it sounds like your dad did, too." She winks at me. "Why don't you take your bag inside and get washed up while I talk to your dad?"

"Okay," Elli says, grabbing her things. "Am I going home with you?"

Heather looks at me, and I nod. "If you'd like to."

Elli's fist comes down to her side. "YES!" She takes the key from my outstretched hand, and runs to unlock the door and head inside.

"Sorry," Heather says sheepishly. "I just wanted to see her, and I knew you'd be home today."

"It's okay," I say, finding that I mean it. "She's missed you."

"I've missed her so much." Heather looks back at the house and turns back to me. "Being away made me realize I don't want to be gone from Elli. I missed so much, even though it was just the end of the school year and part of her summer."

I nod. "I don't like it when I miss out on things in her life, either."

"That's the thing," Heather says, releasing a sigh. "They offered me the junior partnership position, but it would require relocating."

I suck in a breath, ready to go to battle. We agreed when we divorced we wouldn't be more than an hour away from each other. It was important to us that Elli have both her parents close.

Heather holds up her hand to stop me as I open my mouth. "Just listen, okay?"

I snap my mouth closed and nod.

"I couldn't do it. Everything I thought I wanted felt so wrong."

I let out a relieved groan. "Thank you."

Heather smiles sadly. "Yeah, well, I wish I'd known that years ago."

I tilt my head and consider what she said. "Do you think it would have made a difference for us?"

She shakes her head. "I don't think so. We were too different. We wanted to love each other, but I'm not sure we ever did. Not in the right way."

I nod, feeling a bit of resentment lift.

"Besides," she says playfully. "You never had that dreamy look on your face when people talked about us being together."

I dip my head. "I'm sorry, Heather."

She laughs. "It's okay. I'm just glad you're letting yourself move on. I was worried you'd built a wall and would never let anyone back in."

"You know, I thought so too," I admit.

Just then, the front door swings open, and Elli comes rushing out. Her hair dripping wet from the shower, and her little suitcase she uses to go back and forth between my house and Heather's bumping along behind her. "I'm ready," she shouts.

"Come and give me a hug," I say, kneeling down. I squeeze her tight when she steps into my arms. "Be good for your mom, okay?"

"Yeah," she grunts. "You're squeezing me too tight."

I laugh and loosen my grip. "I'm gonna miss you, but I'll see you soon."

"Miss you too, Daddy. Love you."

She squeezes me one last time before pulling away and opening the door to Heather's car.

"Thank you," Heather says, emotion making her voice wobble. "For everything."

"You're welcome," I say. "See you soon."

I stand in the driveway and watch them pull away, Elli waving like mad from the backseat. I wasn't ready for her to go yet. I've been enjoying our summer together.

These are the moments I hate. The time right after Elli goes with her mom, and I feel lost without her.

I unload the truck and take a quick shower. I still promised Reese dinner and a movie, and that sounds a lot better than moping around here alone tonight.

I shoot Reese a text that I'm running late, and pull open the door to Pizza and Playtime. It's busy here tonight. The pizza joint also boasts pool tables and arcade style games, so it's a popular place for teens in the summer.

I step up to the to-go counter. "To-Go order for Daniel Stevens." I tell the teen working the counter. He searches the boxes on the shelves next to him and grabs the large box. "One large pepperoni pizza to go," he says, setting the box down beside the register. "That'll be sixteen dollars even."

I pull out my wallet and hand him a twenty. "Keep the change."

"Thanks, man." He grins and hands me the hot box.

I slide back into the truck, carefully balancing the pizza on the passenger seat, and back out of the space. Excitement for the night ahead flutters through my veins. This will be the first night Reese and I will spend time alone together.

I pull into the small parking lot of Reese's apartment strip and park in one of the spots designated for guests. Grabbing the pizza, I step out of the truck and head to her apartment. I knock on the door and grin when it immediately swings open.

My smile falters and I lean back to check the apartment number again. This is what she said. Confused, I look back at the perfectly kempt older woman standing in the doorway. "Hi," I manage. "Does Reese live here?"

The woman looks me over from head to toe, a polite smile held in place firmly. "I'm sorry," she says curtly. "Who are you?"

I shift the pizza box to my hip and hold out my hand. "Daniel Stevens." I wait a beat for her to shake my hand, letting it drop when it becomes apparent she has no plans to do so.

"And how do you know Reese?"

That smile hasn't slipped once, but I get the feeling I'm failing some test I wasn't aware I was taking. "I'm her boyfriend, ma'am." I shake my head, a bit taken aback. Maybe this is a neighbor who was watching over her place while we were gone?

"Oh," the woman gasps, her hand going to her chest. "I think you must be mistaken," she says, shaking her head with what I can only assume is pity. "Reese doesn't have a boyfriend. I'm her mother, so I'd know."

I stand frozen in place. Her mother? Oh boy.

"Well," I hesitate, unsure how much to say. "It's new, ma'am."

"Mhmm," she grunts. "Well, Reese won't be able to have . . . that with you tonight," she says, waving her hand toward the cooling pizza. "She and I have plans."

"Oh," I say dumbly.

"Daniel!" Reese comes into view. "I see you've met my mother." She grimaces. "She surprised me and came for a visit."

"Oh, how lovely," I say, pasting a smile on my face. "I'll just leave you two to your plans."

Reese frowns. "What plans?" She turns and looks at her mother. "I invited Daniel and Elli over before I even knew you were here." She turns suddenly and peeks around me. "Where's Elli?"

"She's with Heather. She surprised us too," I say, my lips tipping up with the absurdity of the events of the evening.

"Oh, good." Reese lets out a long sigh. "I mean. Not good, but, well, she didn't have to meet my mom like this," she whispers.

"I can hear you, you know," her mom calls. "Who is Elli?" she asks, her tone dripping with disapproval.

"Elli is my daughter, Mrs. Sunderland."

Elli's mom sputters, her face turning several shades of red. "You mean to tell me you're dating a middle-aged man who has a *child!*" she says, her voice rising with every word. "Oh, no. No way." She shakes her head. "What will everyone think? Absolutely not, young lady. This won't do."

My mouth drops open in surprise. I know our age difference and my daughter are a bit of a surprise, but this kind of reaction is over the top.

"Mother!" Reese pleads. "Can we please talk about this later?"

"No way, missy. We are discussing this now. Tell your friend to go home." Her mother stamps her foot like a toddler throwing a tantrum.

"Mother! You're being rude." Reese looks from me to her mom, discomfort lining her features.

"It's okay," I tell her softly. "Talk to your mom. Call me later."

She nods, mouthing "I'm sorry" and closing the door.

I stand in front of the closed door, listening to their muffled voices. What in the world just happened?

I pull my phone out of my pocket and debate calling Evan or Brant. Finally settling on Evan, I search through the contacts until I find his name and hit call.

"What's up, man?" Evan asks, slightly out of breath.

"Uh, you busy? I have a pizza."

"Come on over," he says. "See you soon." He hangs up before I can say goodbye.

A few minutes later, I'm across town and pulling into a parking space in Evan's apartment complex. One of the newer ones with amenities like a pool, and sand volleyball court. It's strange to me that Piney Brook has gotten big enough for an official apartment complex, but apparently it has.

I climb the steps to Evan's second floor apartment and knock on his door. I glance across the hall where a wreath adorns the door on the other side. A cute welcome mat says "Wipe Your Paws" with kitten paws all over it. I chuckle. This must be his new neighbor.

"Hey," Evan says, pulling the door open. His cat, Mittens, snuggled into his chest. "What's up? Didn't you just spend days with me? I mean, I know I'm great and all, but . . ."

He closes the door behind me as I step through and place the pizza on the table to the right. His apartment isn't huge—a small dining area and kitchen open to the living space. A bathroom that has double doorways entering his bedroom on one side, and the hallway on the other round out the space.

"Yeah, yeah," I shrug. "I had plans with Elli and Reese, but . . ."

"But what?" Evan says, stepping into the kitchen and grabbing some paper plates. He passes me one and flips open the lid of the pizza box. "There's Coke, sweet tea, and water in the fridge. Help yourself."

I head to the fridge and grab a Coke. I pop the tab and take a drink.

"But what?" Evan asks again, sitting down with half the pizza in front of him.

"Well, when I got home, Heather was waiting. She came back a week early and missed Elli."

Evan nods, taking a huge bite of pizza as he settles back into his couch. "Okay," he says, his mouth full. "And Reese?"

I grab two slices of pizza and the can of Coke. "I was met at the door by her mother."

Evan looks at me for a second, swallows his food, and then bursts out laughing. "Oh man, how'd that go?"

"Well, I'm here eating cold pizza with you, so . . ."

"Dang, that stinks." He takes another bite of the pizza. "I was just going to watch the game tonight and order pizza anyway. You're welcome to hang out here."

"Thanks," I say, settling back into the couch as he flips the channels before finding the Cardinal's game. I keep checking my phone, waiting for something from Reese. As much as I don't want to get hurt, I really don't want to be in the middle of a mother-daughter issue either. That usually doesn't work out well in the long run.

By eleven, I give up and head home. If I hear from Reese, it won't be tonight. I sigh, and hope that my heart isn't about to be broken.

CHAPTER TWENTY

Reese

"MOTHER," I GRIT OUT, trying to rein my temper in. "That was incredibly rude." I pace the small space in my living room that isn't taken up with her things. "I can't believe you would say such mean things."

"What is incredibly rude is not answering your mother's calls for a week. Not telling me you had a boyfriend is also *incredibly rude.*" She spits the words like a cobra spitting venom.

"I was at the lake—I told you that." I rub the space between my eyebrows, a dull throb is starting to pulse there.

"Yes, and that is another thing." Mom pauses. "Don't you think it's rude to avoid seeing your parents on your vacation?"

"No, Mom, I don't," I grind out. "I wanted to spend one week with my friends. Why is that so awful?"

"Clearly these friends are a bad influence," she says, her face contorted with disgust. "Who would encourage you to date a man with a child? And he is so much older than you."

I shake my head. "They aren't a bad influence, Mom." I sigh and fall down onto the sofa. "I like him, and Elli. They make me happy."

Mom huffs. "Happy! Happy, she says. Happiness is fleeting, Reese. You don't want to be stuck teaching forever. You want to have children, stay at home, be a wife your husband can count on. That is what will make you happy."

I shake my head. "No, Mom. That's what *you* wanted. I love my job, and yes, I'd like to get married and maybe have children someday, but it's not the only thing I want out of life."

"Psh, don't be silly." Mom shakes her head. "How will you ever get out of this little town marrying a man with a child? He is stuck here. STUCK until that child is an adult."

"Why would I want to leave Piney Brook?" I ask, confused. "I've never said I wanted to leave."

"Of course you do," Mom says, taking a seat next to me on the couch. "I know you are happy here now, but this won't be enough. Once you have children, you'll want to be closer to your father and me, to have help."

"How do you know that?" I wait.

"Reese, be serious. Think this through. That man is, what, fifteen years older than you?"

"Ten," I insert.

"Ten, fifteen . . . That's not the point. He already has a child. What makes you think he would want more?"

"We haven't gotten that far, Mom," I say, working hard to keep my voice low.

"Good, then it should be no problem to break it off. Do it now before you hurt that little girl. What will she think if you've been around for a while, and suddenly you're gone? Or worse, what if you have a child with him, and she feels replaced? Would you really want to do that to her?"

I sit back on the couch.

"You need to be with a man your age. One with dreams and aspirations. Someone who you can help move forward in his career. That's what we've always worked towards. Don't lose sight of that now. You may think you're happy, but that fades. How many other boys have caught your attention and then lost it over the years? Now a child is involved."

My stomach hurts. I'd never want to hurt Elli. That sweet girl is precious to me. But the thought of letting Daniel go makes me physically ache. The last few days, I've been the happiest I've ever felt. He made me feel cherished, seen. Important.

"Just think about it, dear." She stands and pats me on the shoulder. "Now, get ready, please; we have dinner plans."

I shake my head. "I'd rather stay in."

"And disappoint our dinner companions? I don't think so. We need to leave in fifteen minutes if we're to make it on time." She makes a shooing motion with her hands.

Reluctantly, I head to my bedroom to change. My head is spinning with how differently this night has turned out. I was so excited to eat pizza and watch a movie with Elli and Daniel.

Fifteen minutes later, I'm climbing into Mom's rental car. "Where are we going?" I ask, staring out the window.

"We are meeting some friends at BlueFin Steakhouse."

I nod.

Thirty minutes later, we're stepping into the elegant restaurant. Rustic lanterns dot the walls, casting a warm hue in the room. Booths line the walls, and smaller, more intimate table settings are spaced around the interior of the room.

"We're meeting the Burnetts," Mom tells the hostess.

"Yes," she says, picking up two menus. "Right this way."

We're led down the aisle toward the back of the room to a circular booth near the kitchen. "Here we are," the hostess says, stepping to the side.

"Gladys, so glad you could make it. You must be Reese." An older woman, dressed in a purple skirt suit, stands and pulls me into a hug. "So happy to meet you."

"Thank you," I say sweetly, trying not to sneeze from the cloud of her perfume.

"I'm Delilah. Let me introduce you to my son, Becket." She gestures to the handsome man standing beside her. "Becket here is a graduate of University of Texas. He's just moved to Bentonville to start work with the Goodman, Fuller, and Waite accounting firm. Isn't that right, Becket?"

"Yes, ma'am," he says to his mom. "Nice to meet you." He extends his hand and I shake it politely. The spark I feel when Daniel touches me is noticeably absent.

"You as well," I manage.

Becket is handsome enough, laughs at all the right things. He has impeccable manners. I'm sure he will make someone a wonderful husband some day. Just not me.

Mother and Delilah keep steering the conversation to the two of us, and how much we have in common. Which is almost nothing.

"Your mother tells me you're a family man," Mom says, elbowing me in the side. "Isn't that lovely? I bet you'd like an entire house full of children."

Becket swallows his steak and smiles politely. "I'd like children one day, yes."

"Reese here is so good with children. She's a preschool teacher now, but has dreams of staying home with her children one day. Isn't that right, dear?"

I choke on my potato.

"Oh, goodness," Mom says, patting my back. "She is so clumsy."

I cringe, still coughing up bits of potato. I don't know what is more humiliating—my mother trying to sell me as wife potential or choking on my food.

The night continues in much the same way until finally I feign exhaustion and remind Mom we have a long ride home.

She gives me her famous side eye, and I know I've been less than impressive tonight. I can't wait to hear all about it in the car. I sigh.

After saying our goodbyes, Mother and I climb into her car. I buckle my seatbelt, and wait for it.

She starts the car, and pulls out of the parking lot, getting back onto the highway before the onslaught finally comes.

"What on earth do you think you were doing in there? You barely even held your end of the conversation," she says, her voice shaking with anger.

"Eating," I reply, knowing it's going to make it worse. I'm just too exhausted by all of this to care.

"I'll be shocked if Becket ever calls you after this. You couldn't manage one meal where you didn't embarrass me or yourself?"

I don't bother to reply.

"How will you ever marry someone decent if you don't even try?" She sighs.

The rest of the ride home is silent. Her fuming, and me wondering if I'll ever make her happy.

The next day, I wake to my mother banging around in my kitchen. I groan as the sound of a cabinet slamming echoes through the apartment.

Pushing the covers back, I crawl out of bed and rub my hands over my face. Here we go again.

Stepping out of the bedroom, I paste a smile on my face. "Good morning, Mother. I trust you slept well." I walk through to the kitchen and grab a coffee mug, pop a pod into the maker, and press start.

"I'd have slept a lot better if you had a proper guest room," she says, haughty.

"You didn't have to come," I remind her. "And I offered you my bed."

"I'm not taking your bed," she huffs.

"Okay . . ." I say, glancing at the half full cup. *Please fill faster.* "Where's Dad?" I ask, barely containing a yip of excitement when the coffee pot sputters signaling the end of the cycle.

"Your father," Mom says pointedly, "is working. As usual."

I nod my head and decide to drink the coffee black today. I take a huge sip, burning my mouth, and thanking the inventor of coffee for the nectar of the morning.

"He's expecting us today."

Coffee spits from my mouth, making a mess on the kitchen floor, and staining my favorite pajamas. "I'm sorry, what?"

"He is expecting us this afternoon. We have to get ready for the Fourth of July gathering. You know how much work that is."

She looks at me as though I've lost my mind. Maybe I have.

"Mom, I can't just leave today. I only got back from the lake yesterday. I have clients tomorrow, and a life." I drop to my knees to wipe up the coffee splattered on the floor.

"Yes, well, reschedule them."

Mom has always been like this. Expecting me to make my schedule work for her. My father is a prominent lawyer in Piney Ridge, and she never misses a chance to attend events she deems beneficial to his career. They started hosting the Fourth of July when I was in elementary school. When everyone else was headed to the city center to see fireworks with their friends, I was stuck at a stuffy business dinner entertaining the other children the way my mom did the wives.

They always hired someone to light off a few fireworks to signal the end of the event, but it was never the kind that my friends talked about.

"I absolutely cannot do that on such short notice. I'm sorry. You'll just have to make do until I can come help with setup this weekend."

"Reese," she says patronizingly. "The weekend doesn't leave us enough time. There's simply too much to be done for you to not come until then."

"Well, then hire someone else, Mom." I've given in so many times, but on this I will not budge. I can't risk my professional reputation by being flighty.

"Fine." She stands from where she'd taken a seat at the table and huffs.

"Mom," I call, trying one last time to figure this out. "What is actually happening here?"

She spins on her heel. "What is actually happening, it seems, is that you don't want anything to do with your family anymore. You never call or come home to visit. You don't even answer your phone when I call. You've resisted every decent boy I've introduced you to. It's like you have no desire to spend time with us, or be near us, anymore. You'd rather be with your new friends."

My mouth drops open in shock. "I don't even know what to say to that."

"Don't say anything," she says furiously, swiping at her eyes. "I'll hire help, and we will see you this weekend. Please pack something appropriate for the event."

I stand stunned as my mother grabs her things and walks out the door. Was she crying?

I rush outside to catch her, but I'm too late. She's pulling out of the parking lot. I grab my phone, turn it back on, and call Anne.

"Hello?" she answers. "Do you know what time it is?"

I smack my forehead. I'd not even considered the hour. "I'm so sorry," I say quickly. "It's an emotional emergency."

"I'll be there in half an hour. Have coffee."

"Thank you," I whisper.

"That's what friends are for." She yawns and hangs up.

Thirty minutes later, I'm still pacing the floor when Anne comes through the door. "I brought donuts. Please tell me you have lots of coffee."

She puts the white pastry box on the counter and takes the cup I hand her.

"So good, thank you. Now, what was the emergency?"

"So, you're telling me you're thinking of breaking it off with the only man who's ever really captured your attention?" Anne pauses and takes another bite of her French cruller. "Because your mom threw a fit."

I drop my head into my hands to hide the tears that are coming again. "I don't know," I say. "I'm so confused. What if it doesn't work out and Elli gets hurt? What if it does work out and she feels replaced, like my mom said? I couldn't live with that."

Anne pins me with a stare. "Reese Sunderland the very fact that you're worried about her feelings means you would handle it carefully. If it doesn't work out, then you explain it's not her, and if Daniel and Heather allow it, remain a part of her life."

"Okay, but ..."

"No buts," she says, waving the last bite of donut at me. "If it does work out, you will make her feel nothing less than loved and cherished. Reese, you have a huge heart, and you always put others first. Even when they don't deserve it."

I shake my head. "I don't know."

Several hours later, I still haven't decided what the right thing to do is. I need time.

CHAPTER TWENTY-ONE

Daniel

I WOKE UP THIS morning thinking I'd have a missed call or text from Reese. Something to give me a clue what's going on. The more I think about it, the more upset I become. Heather's parents were always interfering in our relationship, and I let them. I think it was easier to go with the flow than to cause a stir.

Reese's mom made it pretty clear that she wasn't on board with Reese dating an older single father. At first, I was pretty peeved to be written off without a backwards glance. Then I began to wonder how I'd feel if Elli came home with a divorced older man with a family.

I'd like to say I'd be fine with it, as long as she was happy and the man treated her right. But I just don't know.

Evan told me to give Reese some space to work her stuff out, and he's right. I just didn't anticipate how hard it would be to give her space now that my heart's gone all in.

When I walk into work, Evan gives me a knowing nod, keeping his usual banter to himself. Weird.

Brant comes out of the office shortly after I get my head under the first car of the day. "Hey, Daniel," he says, pulling me from my work.

"Hey."

"Can you come into the office for a minute and help me with something?" he asks.

"Sure." I wipe my hands on a shop towel, and follow him into the office. "What's up?"

Brant points to the chair in front of him. "Well, it's probably nothing," he starts. "Morgan called Reese this morning to make sure she'd be there for the Fourth. Reese said she'd be at her parents' house for the holiday. Morgan thinks she'd been crying."

I drop my head into my hands. I guess I have my answer.

"What's going on?

I blow out a breath and start from the beginning.

"Wow," Brant says, lacing his fingers together on the desk. "I don't know what to say. And she hasn't contacted you since?"

I shake my head. "Nope."

"Have you tried to call her?" he asks.

"No, I was giving her space. The last thing I want to do is make her life harder. I also don't want to be in another relationship where the parents have more say about what is happening than the people involved." I sigh. "This is why I didn't want to open up, you know."

Brant sits quietly. "I wouldn't go counting anything out without talking to her first. She was as all in as you were."

I let out a sad laugh. "I thought so too."

After leaving Brant's office, I call Heather to make sure she knows to take Elli to tutoring today. She reassures me she's got this under control, and not to worry so much. Ha!

I make it through the rest of the week without calling Reese and demanding answers, but just barely. I told myself I'd give her space. I left the ball in her court when I left her apartment.

Saturday morning, I'm still in my pajamas when Heather brings Elli for the weekend. I thought about seeing if Heather wanted to keep her this weekend, but I've never skipped my weekend with Elli, and I'm not going to start now.

"You look awful," Heather says, sitting Elli's bag down in the foyer. "Elli, why don't you head out back and play. Give me a minute with your dad."

"Kay!" Elli shouts, running outside.

"That was harsh," I say, running my hand through my hair.

Heather puts her hands on her hips. "Well, look at yourself." She points to the coffee table; several dishes are stacked on the surface. "She still hasn't called?" She makes her way to the other end of the sofa, pushing piles of clean clothes over so she can sit down.

"No, and I don't think she will." I look around at the mess I've let pile up all week. I'm better than this. I didn't even let it get this bad during the divorce.

"I know you think she's cut you out, but I can tell you she looks almost as bad as you do. Or she did on Thursday when I picked Elli up from tutoring."

I stand, picking up the dirty plates, and take them to the kitchen sink. "I don't want to know," I say firmly. "I can't do this, Heather. I can't get my heart broken again."

Heather comes into the kitchen carrying a few cups. "Do you care for her?"

I place my hands on the edge of the sink and sigh, my head falling to my chest. "I do, so much."

She nods. "Then you need to decide if it's better to let her go without a fight, or fight for the kind of love you've always wanted. I see it in your eyes when you talk about her. Don't answer, just think about it."

I nod. Heather steps outside to say goodbye to Elli, and pauses on her way back through the house. "I'll come get her Sunday night. Call me if you need me to come before that."

A few hours later, my phone rings, and I jump to answer it. A moment of disappointment washes over me when I see it's my mom, not Reese.

"Hey, Ma," I say, answering the phone.

"What's this I hear about a girlfriend?" Her excitement is palpable, even through the phone.

I groan. "Elli called you?" I ask, already knowing the answer.

"She did, a few days ago. I've been waiting to see if you'd call me and tell me about her. When can I meet her?"

I wipe my hand down my face and let out a breath. "Well . . ." I sigh.

"Oh no," Mom whispers. "No, it's not ended already, has it? Elli was so excited about her."

"I really don't know what is happening." I'd like to reassure Mom, but honestly, I have no clue what to think. Especially since she hasn't reached out to me.

"It's the weekend. You have Elli, right?" Mom asks.

"Yeah," I sigh. "I don't have plans until about four. Brant and Morgan invited me to their place for dinner. I think they feel sorry for me."

"Come on over, dear. I have some fresh blueberry muffins and coffee. Besides, I need your help in the garden."

"All right, Ma." I grab my keys from the hook by the door. "I'm on my way."

Twenty minutes later, I'm standing on Mom's porch, coffee in hand, listening to her talk about her gardening project. Elli is checking each snapdragon and marigold she planted before the lake trip.

"So if you could just help me dig that space up and replant it, that would be great." Mom says drawing my attention away from Elli.

I shake my head. "Do you have the plants?"

"Well, no. I hadn't really thought we'd do it today, but you need something to keep those hands and that mind of yours busy. You just opened yourself up, and there seems to be some doubt about how that is going to go."

I sigh. "Mom. I'm fine."

"Yeah, well, you will be. Because it's all going to work out. Don't you worry." She grins and pats my shoulder. "In the meantime, help an old lady out."

I sigh and roll up my sleeves. No sense in arguing.

Several hours later, we have the area cleared out and tilled. I'm exhausted and filthy.

"We can finish another day," Mom says, patting my cheek. "You've got a dinner to get to."

Monday morning, I debate telling Brant I'm not going to make it. Remembering the mess Heather and Elli found me in Saturday morning, I decide to go. I can't help but hope Reese will be there tonight. When we left the lake house, that had been her plan. It's hard not to feel like she's going to her parents' to avoid me.

I pull into Brant's driveway and a pang of disappointment settles into my chest. Her car isn't here. Sighing, I step out of the truck and make my way to the festivities in the back yard. Elli was supposed to be here tonight, but Heather asked if she could spend the time with her instead, since she's been gone all summer and I said yes. Now I wish I'd brought her along.

Morgan is standing with Susan and some other women I recognize from the wedding. Probably fellow teachers.

I spot Evan and Brant with Susan's husband, Sam, and head in that direction.

"Hey, Daniel," Sam says. "Nice to see you again."

"You too," I say, sending him what I hope looks like a friendly smile. "Need any help?" I ask Brant.

"Nah," he says, pointing to the cooler. "Help yourself. We'll start the grill up in a little bit, but there are appetizers in the house if you want some. Something called a charcuterie board, whatever that means. It's basically cheese and crackers." He shrugs.

Sam laughs. "Don't let Susan hear you say that. She has a whole magazine full of ideas for those things."

Evan pops a cube of cheese into his mouth. "I don't care what you call it, I love these things."

I shake my head, and walk over to the cooler. Pulling out a bottle of water, I look around the back yard again, hoping I'm wrong and she's here after all. No such luck.

I join some guys I don't know at the corn hole setup and introduce myself. I team up with Bethany's husband, Aiden, and spend some time getting lost in conversation. After losing a second time, I beg off and find Brant at the grill.

"How ya holding up?" he asks. "Has she called you yet?"

I shake my head. Unable to make the words come out. "Can I help you with anything?"

Brant looks at me for a minute, but then lets it go. "Sure. Want to grab the chicken from the refrigerator?"

"You got it." I step inside the house and take a minute to soak in the quiet. Making my way to the fridge, I take out the bowl of chicken and snag another bottle of water. "Here you go," I say, setting the chicken down on the fold-out table Brant's using as a prep station.

"Thanks, man." He flips the burgers already on the grill and steps back. "What's your plan?"

"What do you mean?" I take a sip of water and lean back against the side of the house.

"Well, how long are you going to give her space before you fight for her?" Brant asks, pinning me with a stare.

"What are you talking about?" I shake my head. "We were only dating for a few days."

Brant shakes his head and mutters something under his breath. "You may have been official for a few days, but you've been falling for each other for months."

I open my mouth to deny it, but nothing comes. He's right. The times I've spent getting to know her as friends have been some of the best of my life. Images of her playing the made-up card game with Elli and me at the kitchen table fill my mind.

"You're right," I say, my shoulders sagging. "How did I miss that?"

"You weren't looking for love. It found you." Brant shrugs. "So, what is your plan?"

"I don't know." I hesitate. "What if I fight for her and lose?" I shake my head. "I'm not sure my heart can take it."

Brant nods. "True—that's a possibility."

"Thanks, man," I say sarcastically.

"Or," he says, pointing his tongs at me. "What if you fight for her and you win the best thing that's ever happened to you, aside from Elli?"

"I'll think about it." I hand Brant the platter to put the burgers on, and wait while he fills it up. When he's done, I cover the whole thing with foil to keep it hot and the flies away.

"Don't take too long," he warns.

"Yeah," I say. What would it mean to fight for her? I don't want to make her relationship with her parents rocky, but I also know that we have something special. I'm not ready to just walk away from that.

I spend the rest of the afternoon waiting for sunset and mingling with the people Brant and Morgan invited. I've been mulling over a plan to fight for Red.

We were fine before her mom surprised her. So that's where I'll need to start—with her parents. If I haven't heard from Reese by tomorrow afternoon, I'm driving up to her parents' place. They may never give me their approval, but I have to try. For her.

Chapter Twenty-Two

Reese

"Hi, Daddy," I say, leaning down to kiss my father's cheek. "How are you today?" I ask before sitting down beside him.

"Just fine, Reese," he says, patting my leg. "How are you? You've seemed mopey since you got here the other day."

"I'm all right. Just thinking some things through." I don't want to get into it here, and definitely not with my dad. We've never been close like that. He's always been working.

He nods his head and takes a sip from his rocks glass. "I see."

His co-workers and their wives are seated at the long tables set up under the white canopy. The buffet is set up against the far side of the tent, allowing ample room for mingling. A drink station, complete with a bartender, is in the corner, out of the way of the activity.

"I thought I'd wait by you until the line dies down to get some food." I sigh, and my fingers find the hem of my blouse.

"Does this thinking you're doing have anything to do with your gentleman friend?"

I gasp. "Daddy!" I say, quietly. "What has Mother told you?"

"Only that she stepped in just in time. Something about finding you with a gentleman caller who was much too old for you. A single father at that."

I groan and bury my face in my hands. "Can we not talk about this now?" I beg.

"I'm afraid if I don't talk to you now, while your mother is busy, I won't get a chance." He sighs. "You have to understand your mom." He looks at me for a moment before glancing away again and clearing his throat. "We tried so hard to have kids, and months turned into years before we were finally blessed with you. She switched her focus to helping me get ahead, and I think she was a bit afraid of being a mom at that point."

"Dad, I really don't think . . ."

He pats my leg. "Let me finish, please." He takes another drink from the tumbler in his hand. "She's always tried to make sure you had the best of everything. When it looked like I could get a promotion, she doubled down on social events and proving to everyone around that I deserved it. I tried to tell her it wasn't necessary, but she was determined that nothing hold you back from the life you deserved."

My eyes find Mom in the crowd and, for the first time, I try to understand her.

"She wants you to marry someone your own age who doesn't already have children because she thinks it's the only way you'll have a shot at the family you've always wanted. She doesn't want you to struggle like we did."

A tear slides down my face, and I wipe at it with my cocktail napkin. "Daddy, I just want to be happy."

He pats my leg. "That's all we want for you, too, Reese. Deep down, that's what your mom wants. She just doesn't know how to show it sometimes. Does this man make you happy?"

"He does, Dad. He treats me like I matter. Like he sees me. The real me, not the mess I can sometimes be."

"You're not a mess, darlin'." Dad turns towards me. "You're perfect just the way you are. Any man who doesn't see that isn't worth your time."

"Thanks, Daddy," I say, leaning in to hug him.

"If this man means as much to you as I think he does, you should be with him tonight, not here with your old dad." He leans his shoulder into me. "Go, I'll talk to your mother."

Hope blooms in my chest. "What if it's too late? It's already been a week, and Mom said some things that were pretty unkind. I didn't defend him. What if he doesn't want to take a chance with me?"

Dad shakes his head. "Reese, there's nothing that could keep a man away if he's the right one for you." He chuckles to himself. "Not even your mom when she's in one of her snits. Now, go, before you lose your chance to slip out."

I jump to my feet, place a kiss on Dad's cheek, and hustle my way into the house and out the front door to my car.

The drive to Morgan's is just under an hour, giving me way too much time to think about all the ways this could go wrong.

What If he isn't even there?

My nerves are on fire by the time I reach Piney Brook city limits. I pull off to the side of the road and take a few deep breaths. "You can do this. You can do this," I repeat until I finally feel ready to drive again.

A few minutes later, I sag in relief when I spy Daniel's truck in the driveway. I touch the door as I walk by, hoping I'm not about to make a huge fool out of myself. Noise from the back yard captures my attention, and make my way through the side yard to the party. I spot Morgan first, standing with some of the other teachers from work.

Morgan smiles and waves me over, but I shake my head. If I stop now, I'll lose my nerve. I stand in the shadows and scan the back yard. Strings of lights are hung all across the yard, creating a warm glow. They give off just enough light to see by. There's a corn hole game going, and a stack of fireworks on a small table in the middle of the yard.

My palms are starting to feel damp, so I wipe them on my slacks. The polyester reminds me that I'm way overdressed for this event. I'd have stopped to change, but the sun was already setting, and I didn't want to lose any more time.

Brant steps up to the table and hands Liam a sparkler, lighting it with a punk. Liam giggles and waves the sparkler around. Other kids line up for their sparklers, and their laughter echoes in the yard. I watch for a moment, caught up in their joy.

The sliding glass door opens, and I feel him before I see him. My heart jackhammers in my chest. It's now or never. I step out of the shadows and into the dim lighting of the back yard. He's standing with his back to me. His jeans fit him like a second skin. I swallow and take another step forward. It's now or never.

"Daniel," I call. His back goes stiff and he holds absolutely still. I clear my throat nervously. "Daniel," I try again. This time he turns. Slowly scanning the area as though he can't believe what he's hearing. Finally, his eyes find mine, and a smile lights up his face.

He rushes to me, and hugs me tight. "I didn't think you were coming."

"I wasn't," I whisper. "Can we talk?"

He pulls back and searches my face, his brow furrowed in concern. "Of course. Let's step over here. The fireworks will still be a few minutes. It should be quiet enough."

I nod and follow him up the steps and into a quiet corner of the back porch. Daniel puts his hand on my lower back and guides me to the railing.

I lean back on my elbows against the wooden supports, and really drink him in. He stands in front of me, his thumbs in his front pockets. I want him to close the space, but I understand why he doesn't.

"What do you want to talk about?" he says warily, giving me the space to talk first.

His eyes drift to the people mingling in the back yard before he pins them back on me. I shiver, and wrap my hands around my middle, trying to ground myself.

"I owe you an apology," I say, looking at my hands. "My mom .. . ever since I was little, she's had big plans. Plans I let her think I shared because it was easier than trying to get her to listen." I look at him, taking a moment to collect my thoughts.

"She and my father had a hard time starting a family, and I didn't understand her motivations then, but I am starting to. She thinks I need to accomplish certain things, live a certain life, to be fulfilled." I take a deep breath and slowly let it out.

He reaches out and takes my hand. "I can understand that," he says softly. "I want Elli to have the best life she can."

I nod. "I'm so sorry she acted like that when you met her. I was so overwhelmed from finding her in my house when I got back that I didn't even think about how that would go. I'm just so grateful Elli wasn't there." I sigh. "I should have handled that better, and not shut you out. I needed some time to think."

"I'm glad Elli wasn't there, too," he says, rubbing his thumb across my knuckles. "I'll understand if you don't want to pursue a relationship with me. I can't say I haven't thought about the fact that I'm older than you, or that I have a child from a previous relationship. That is a lot to take on. Before spending time with you, I wasn't sure if I'd ever be open to having more children. I was afraid to let you in, because you deserve everything, Reese."

A tear slips from the corner of my eye. This is so much harder than I thought it would be. "I have always wanted children of my own one day, but Elli has a special place in my heart. She is the sweetest girl, and I've grown to really care about her." I pause, attempting to gather my courage. "Almost as much as I care about her father."

Daniel's hand stills on mine. "What did you say?"

"I said I am falling for you, and, try as I might, I can't stop it. I don't want to stop it. I want to be in this with you. All the way." I pull my hand from his and place it on the side of his face. "I'm falling in love with you, Daniel, and if you're still willing to give this a shot, I am too. I can't promise that my mom won't ever overstep, or that I'll always say or do the right thing. I can only promise that I'll try my best, and always talk things through."

"No more ghosting me for a week?" he asks.

I shake my head. "That was the hardest week of my life. I thought I was protecting you, and Elli, but really I was just afraid of what loving someone this much might mean."

"I love you, Reese. I have since I saw you throw that fish back into the lake." Daniel leans his forehead against mine. "Reese Sunderland, will you be my girlfriend?"

I giggle, the word seemingly too small for how I feel for this man. "Yes." My mom may struggle with this, but I've never felt so sure about anything in my life. Daniel is meant for me.

Daniel lets out a whoop and gathers me in his arms. He pulls me in for a kiss, just as the first boom of the fireworks sounds.

Hand in hand, we walk out to the back yard to see the colorful lights. Morgan catches my eye and smiles before leaning her head into Brant's shoulder.

Liam rushes to Daniel, grinning. "Wait till I tell Elli!" he shouts.

"Tell her what?" Brant asks, moving closer.

"That it worked! We made a wish on the wishing flower that Mr. Daniel and Ms. Reese would fall in love. Wishes do come true!" Liam says, shaking his head before turning back to where Evan is setting up the next round of fireworks. Evan's in charge of the light show and is putting on a beautiful display. The explosions and sparkling lights match the way I feel inside with Daniel's hand in mine, and our future ahead of us.

Liam's right, wishes really do come true.

CHAPTER TWENTY-THREE

Daniel

TWO MONTHS LATER

I've checked my pocket a thousand times since Elli and I left to pick Reese up from her apartment this morning. The family heirloom is burning a hole in my pocket. It's Friday afternoon, and we're spending the weekend at the lake since it's a three-day weekend for Labor Day.

"I can't believe you rented this huge house for just us," Reese says, casting her line into the lake. "It's sad no one else could make it. I was looking forward to getting everyone back here together."

"I love this cabin," I say nonchalantly. "It's where we started to fall in love. Plus, I talked to Brant and Evan about coming back to the lake this summer. I think they're in." I agree, having our friends together at the lake was one of the best vacations I've ever had.

"If you catch a fish, are you going to kiss Daddy?" Elli pipes in.

Reese and I laugh. "I hope so," I say, shooting her a wink.

Elli giggles. I'm surprised she hasn't given away our plan. I wanted Elli to feel as much a part of this as Reese and I. She's been so excited to help me plan. Even talking to Reese's parents on the phone a few times. Once her mom realized how much I love Reese, she was on board.

"That kiss was one of the best days of my life," I say, patting my pocket for the hundredth time.

Reese grins. "Mine too," she says, softly.

I look down at my watch, trying not to give anything away. Everyone should be in place soon. I've arranged for our friends and families here for the big moment, but Reese doesn't know it yet. I can't wait to surprise her in front of everyone. I just hope I'm not wrong, and she will be as excited as I am.

"I've got one!" Elli yells, slowly reeling in her line. "I can't believe it! I caught the first fish *again!*" Elli pulls in the small fish and grins, holding it up for us to see. "Not too big, but that's okay."

"Great job," I say, giving her a high five. "You'll be a pro angler before long." I step in, unhook the fish from the line, and toss it back into the lake.

"Was that dinner you just threw in the lake?" a deep voice calls from behind us.

Reese whips around, confusion clear on her face. "Daddy?"

"Hey, baby girl," he says, pausing for a moment. "Sorry we're late."

I grin. "Not late at all," I say, meeting him halfway and shaking his hand. Convincing her parents that I was in love with their daughter and worthy of her love took some time, but it was worth it to have them here today.

"What's going on?" Reese asks, looking between her father and me.

"You-hoo," her mother calls as she rounds the corner of the house. "Did I hear something about a fish?"

Reese's mouth drops open. "Mom?"

"Well, don't look so surprised dear. Daniel invited us to spend the weekend here at the lake with you. We thought it was high time we got to spend some time with Elli." Her eyes find Elli's and she smiles. "How will we ever be able to spoil her if we don't get to see her?"

"You invited them?" she asks. "And you came?"

I nod. "And," I start, but I'm cut off.

"There you are," my mom calls, waving. "I was afraid I'd missed it."

I drop my head into my hand. "Mom, you haven't missed anything except Elli catching the first fish."

"Well, thank goodness for that," she says, smoothing down her bohemian style skirt.

"Grandma," Elli giggles. "You'll give it away."

Reese's eyes ping-pong between her parents, my mom, Elli, and me. "Is anyone going to tell me what's going on here? Give what away?"

All eyes focus on me as I drop to one knee and pull out my mother's wedding band. "Reese Sunderland, since the moment I met you, I haven't been able to get you out of my mind. You've shown me love in a way that I never thought I'd be blessed enough to experience. You've stepped in and loved Elli like she's your own, and every moment I'm with you, you make me a better man."

A choked sound comes from someone behind us. Probably my mom. She was so emotional when I told her I was planning to propose.

Reese gasps and grips the hem of her shirt. "Daniel, what on earth . . ." she whispers.

"I know your parents mean the world to you, so having their blessing was important to me." I nod to her father. "It took some convincing, but I think I've gotten it?" I ask, looking at Mrs. Sunderland.

"You do," she says, wiping a tear from her eye. "We're honored to have you join our family."

I turn back to Reese. "Elli and I would be overjoyed if you would consider spending the rest of your life with us. Will you marry me?"

"This is where you say yes," Elli shouts excitedly before my mother shushes her.

"Yes," Reese says softly. "Yes, I'll marry you!"

I stand just in time to catch her as she jumps into my arms. "I love you," I whisper.

"I love you too," she says before hopping back to her feet and holding out her left hand.

I slip the ring on her finger. "It's not a traditional ring, but it's the one my dad proposed to my mom with, and they had many years of love together."

Reese stares down at the white gold band, a round emerald stone surrounded by little diamonds making it look like a flower. "It's beautiful," she says, holding it up for her mom to see.

"I'm so glad you followed your heart, Reese," Gladys says, pulling her in for a hug. "I've only ever wanted the best for you. I'm sorry if I got a little out of control. Forgive me?"

"Of course, Mom," Reese says, pulling her in tighter.

"Are you supposed to kiss or something?" Elli asks, breaking the tension.

"The girl's right," Mom pipes in.

I gently tug Reese close to me and lean in, placing my lips on hers just as fireworks erupt behind us.

Reese pulls back, and looks toward the lake where all of our friends are standing. Evan holds up the long lighter and waves. "Didn't think we'd miss this did you?"

Reese giggles and it's the best sound I've ever heard.

"You are sneaky," she says, laughing. "I have no idea how you pulled this off."

Brant claps me on the shoulder. "I think we're even now," he says with a wink.

Reese is grinning as she shows off her ring. The women have formed a circle, already discussing wedding dates and plans.

"Does it make you nervous?" Evan asks, pointing to the women. "They're deciding your future over there."

"Nah," I say honestly. "My future isn't the wedding, it's the marriage."

Evan laughs before walking off to join the kids who've made their way down to the shoreline and started skipping rocks.

I watch as Reese basks in the attention of her friends and family, and know that whatever our wedding looks like, it's waking up next to her for the rest of my life that matters.

Epilogue

TEN YEARS LATER

"I think that's the last one," Heather says, stuffing the cardinal and white duffel into Elli's trunk. "I didn't think we'd get it all in."

"Mom," Elli laughs. "Between Dad's truck, your car, and mine, I think we've got it covered."

I watch the interaction, knowing moments like these are going to become more and more rare. "Ready to go, Elli girl?" I ask, needing to change the direction of the conversation before I get emotional. "We're burning daylight."

"Yep." She turns and looks back at the house. "I'm gonna miss you guys."

Reese comes down the front steps, a container in her hands. "Don't forget your snickerdoodles!" She passes the container to Elli and smiles. "We'll be up to visit once you're settled in. We'll give it a few weeks."

Elli grins, and a tear slides down her cheek. "Are you sure you're not going to come?"

Reese leans in and pulls Elli into a bear hug. "Nope, this one is for your mama and daddy," she whispers just loud enough that Heather and I both hear her.

Elli squeezes her back, and then kneels down, pulling Rhett and Clay in for a hug. "Y'all be good for Mom and Dad, okay?" she says, letting them go.

The twins nod their heads solemnly. "Are you sure you have to go?" Rhett, the more talkative of the boys, asks.

Elli lets out a deep breath and pulls them in again. "I have to go learn how to be a good teacher like your mom. That way, I can come back here and help kids like me who have a hard time with reading and math."

In third grade, we had Elli assessed for learning differences. Turns out she's mildly dyslexic and also has dyscalculia. She's worked hard to get where she is today, and I couldn't be more proud of her. My baby is eighteen, and going off to college.

I rub at the ache starting to bloom under my sternum. Time sure does fly.

"All right, boys, we'll be seeing her in a few weeks for family weekend." I step in and ruffle their curly red hair. There was a time I thought I didn't want any more children. I glance at Reese who is shooing the boys back inside with the promise of seeing Levi and Mason this afternoon.

Once the boys are inside, she closes the door and comes to stand beside me. "You're going to do great," she tells Elli, tears streaming down her face. "Don't forget to call us at least once a week and make good choices."

She may not be Elli's biological mom, but there's never been a moment's doubt that she loves her like her own.

Heather steps forward and puts an arm around Reese's shoulders. "We did it," she says proudly. "Our girl is headed to college."

Reese grins and wipes the tears away. "We did."

"All right, seriously," I choke out. "It's time to go." I pull Reese in for a hug and kiss before stepping back and pointing to the cars. "Load up."

Dropping Elli off at college was a mess. Freshman everywhere, families looking lost and confused. By the time we figured out where her dorm was and got everything unloaded, it was getting late. Heather booked a hotel room down the road and is taking Elli out for dinner tonight—one last mother-daughter date.

I'm barely in the driveway when the boys come running out. "Did Elli get moved in?" Rhett asks as I'm getting out of the truck.

"She did." I motion for them to head inside and follow behind them.

"Mom's been acting weird," Clay says, looking down at his feet. "She's been laughing and crying all day."

I nod and put my hand on his shoulder. "Sending your babies off into the world isn't easy. Give her some grace."

The boys nod and head back to the living room and their abandoned video game.

"Reese," I call when I don't see her in the main part of the house. "I'm home."

"In here," she calls.

I follow the sound of her voice into our bedroom and sit down on the bed. *What a day.* "I'm exhausted," I call through the closed bathroom door. "Who knew moving your kid into a dorm room would be so difficult?"

The door slowly opens, and Reese pokes her head out, her eyes red and puffy. I shoot to my feet and go to her. "Babe," I say soothingly, holding her close. "It's okay. We'll see her soon." I knew Reese was feeling emotional about Elli heading to college, but this seems like a lot, even for her. I rub my hands up and down her arms. "She'll be back for Thanksgiving before you know it."

Reese shakes her head, and the tears start to fall. "That's—" she hiccups. "That's not it," she says on a sob.

"Okay," I draw out. "Then what is it? Whatever it is, it can't be that bad." I'm baffled. When I left this morning, the most dramatic thing happening was dropping my daughter off at the University of Arkansas.

Reese pulls me into the bathroom and points to the counter. My breath catches in my throat. "Is that . . .?" I ask, unable to get the sentence out.

She nods.

Carefully, I reach out and pick up the piece of plastic resting on the bathroom counter. *Pregnant.* I turn and pin Reese with a stare, my mouth hanging open in shock. "Baby, are you—? Are we—?"

She nods again, tears streaming down her face. "Yes."

I drop the plastic stick and swing her up into my arms. "I'm gonna be a daddy again!" I shout.

Reese laughs, "You're not upset?"

"Upset?" I ask, setting her back on her feet. "Never." We tried for a while before we were able to have the boys, and when pregnancy number two didn't seem to follow, we resigned ourselves to the idea of three kids. "This is the best surprise ever!"

"We should call Elli and tell her." Reese looks relieved now that she's told me the news. "She'll be upset if she isn't the first to know."

I shake my head. "Uh-uh, I'm not telling her first. She'll have told everyone before we get the chance. Let's call our parents first, then we can tell her."

Reese laughs and playfully slaps my arm. "You're bad," she says. "But you're also right."

Reese grabs her phone and dials the number, putting the phone on speaker. "Reese, dear, I didn't expect to hear from you today, what with Elli leaving. Is everything alright?"

Reese reaches for my hand. "Mom, I have some news." Reese sucks in a breath. "I'm pregnant!"

There's a pause before excited shouts erupt on the other end of the line. "What's all the shouting for?" her dad asks.

"Reese is pregnant!" her mother shouts.

"Gladys, I'm sure that's ... what?"

"Reese and Daniel are going to have another baby!" Gladys says, emotion making her voice thick. "Oh, you two. You've made me the happiest Grammy in the world! We're so happy for you both."

"Why is Grammy yelling?" Clay asks, poking his head into our room.

"Because you're going to be a big brother," I say, my cheeks aching from smiling so big.

"Rhett!" Clay yells as he turns to walk back down the hallway. "Mom's getting another baby. I hope it's a boy."

Reese and I lock eyes and laugh.

After we hang up with Reese's parents, we call my mom and sister. They're just as excited as Gladys was. My cheeks hurt from smiling so much.

"You ready to tell Elli?" Reese asks, handing me the phone.

I nod and punch in her number, making sure to put it on speaker again.

"Hey, Reese, I thought you'd give me at least until tomorrow before you called."

Reese laughs. "We have something to tell you, actually."

She smiles at me and I grin. "You're going to be a big sister again," I say, laughing. Shortly after we had Rhett and Clay, her mom remarried and had another little girl—Emmaline—so Elli gets lots of practice at being the big sister. She's a pro.

"Really?" Elli shouts into the phone. "And I'm going to miss everything," she says. The sound of her sniffling breaks my heart.

"No way," Reese says firmly. "You'll be here on your breaks. Besides, there's always facetime."

After a few more minutes, while Reese grilled Elli about whether she had enough food and money, we finally hang up.

I put my hand on Reese's stomach and grin. "I love you, Reese. Thank you for being my wife. Our babies are so lucky to have you as a mommy." I place a gentle kiss on her lips. This is the life I've always wanted.

If you enjoyed Daniel and Reese's story, I'd love it if you would consider leaving a review on Amazon, Goodreads, or BookBub! It always brings a smile to my face when I read a new review!

Book 3 features Evan and Karlee. Neither one is looking for a relationship, but when the girl next door catches his eye, Evan can't help but fall for her. Read Evan and Karlee's story in Book 3: Wishing for the Girl Next Door available now on Amazon and included in Kindle Unlimited. https://tinyurl.com/WFTGND

Did you miss book 1 in the series? Start at the beginning and read His Christmas Wish, Brant and Morgan's story. Available on

Amazon and included in Kindle Unlimited. https://tinyurl.com/Hi sChristmasWishZon

Curious how Reese *wanted* to react to her mother and Ms. Becky's meddling? Join my newsletter and get access to an alternate scene. https://tinyurl.com/SSWCutScene

Also By Tia Marlee

Piney Brook Wishes Series
His Christmas Wish
Sweet Summertime Wishes
Wishing for the Girl Next Door
A Soldier's Wish

The Coffee Loft Series
Bean Wishing for a Latte Love
You Mocha Me Crazy

About the Author

Tia Marlee resides in Central Texas with her husband and three teenaged children. When she isn't writing, Tia enjoys reading, embroidery and spending time with her family. Tia is the author of the Piney Book Wishes series featuring unexpected love stories based in small-town Piney Brook, Arkansas.

Connect with Tia Marlee
Newsletter: https://www.tiamarlee.com
Facebook: https://tinyurl.com/FBTiaMarlee
Instagram: https://tinyurl.com/IGTiaMarlee
Facebook Group: https://tinyurl.com/TiaMarleeReaderGroup
Amazon: https://tinyurl.com/AmazonTiaMarlee
Goodreads: https://tinyurl.com/GRTiaMarlee
Bookbub: https://tinyurl.com/BBTiaMarlee

Acknowledgements

Thank you to the readers who have taken a chance on a new author. I'll be forever grateful.

To my husband and children who have cheered me on every step of the way. Late nights writing and editing would have been miserable without your support.

To all of my writer friends, especially my accountability group, thank you! You've pushed me to be a better writer, and a better human being.

Printed in Great Britain
by Amazon

49242205R10121